I0534083

Onward
&
Upward

The Angels are Everywhere Series

Books by Linda Hudson Hoagland
from Jan-Carol Publishing, Inc:

THE LINDSAY HARRIS MURDER MYSTERY SERIES:
SNOOPING CAN BE DANGEROUS
SNOOPING CAN BE CONTAGIOUS
SNOOPING CAN BE DEVIOUS
SNOOPING CAN BE DOGGONE DEADLY

THE BEST DARN SECRET
MISSING SAMMY

THE ANGELS ARE EVERYWHERE SERIES:
ONWARD & UPWARD

Onward
&
Upward

The Angels are Everywhere Series

LINDA HUDSON HOAGLAND

Jan-Carol
Publishing, Inc
"every story needs a book"

ONWARD & UPWARD
LINDA HUDSON HOAGLAND

Published October 2015
Little Creek Books
Imprint of Jan-Carol Publishing, Inc
All rights reserved
Copyright © 2015 by Linda Hudson Hoagland

This is a work of fiction. Any resemblance to actual persons, either living or dead is entirely coincidental. All names, characters and events are the product of the author's imagination.

This book may not be reproduced in whole or part, in any matter whatsoever without written permission, with the exception of brief quotations within book reviews or articles.

ISBN: 978-1-939289-76-6
Library of Congress Control Number: 2015955288

You may contact the publisher:
Jan-Carol Publishing, Inc
PO Box 701
Johnson City, TN 37605
publisher@jancarolpublishing.com
jancarolpublishing.com

To My Sons
Michael E. Hudson
Matthew A. Hudson

AUTHOR'S NOTE

Dear Reader,

This is a fictional journey through the life of Molly Thompson; a wanderer, a crocheter, and a believer in the existence of angels. She has never been accused of being shy, but when she reached that sixty plus mark, she made it a point to express her heartfelt opinion about any wrongdoings over which she had the slightest bit of influence. In other words, she doesn't mince words if she feels you have done something wrong.

Molly keeps an eye out for her friends and for strangers when she feels the need and sometimes those friends keep a watchful eye out for her, especially when an event from her past becomes unfinished business and she must fight to see the sun rise again.

This books shares Molly's angel influence life with anyone who believes in angels.

I hope you enjoy reading this novel as much as I enjoyed writing it.

Sincerely,

Linda Hoagland

MY ANGEL

I want angels around me
To help me find the best way
For me to live and to share
With others every day.

Those delicate flying ones
With haloes above their heads,
Protect without our knowing
While we sleep in our safe beds.

My angel is not a beam
Of awesome light; she is good
And tries, much to my delight,
To push me on when she should.

If angels can be just plain,
That is what she is for me.
Radiating her beauty
Would probably make me flee.

I need to be led by one
Who is my equal in life.
Reaching for what I can't be
Causes me much pain and strife.

My guardian angel is
A reflection of how I
See me when it comes a time
For me to leave earth and fly.

CHAPTER 1
CREATING MY FIRST ANGELS

"I want one in baby pink," said the excited young lady, as she rubbed the turquoise afghan laying on the display table in front of her.

"I don't have one with me. I would have to make it. When would you need it?" I asked, trying not to show my skepticism.

"Not for a couple of months. It's for my sister's baby, and I don't know the exact date," she said.

"I can make the angel for you. It will be about a month before I get it finished. Let me have your phone number and name, and I will call you when it is ready. If need be, I can mail it to you," I explained, half-heartedly.

I didn't like taking orders from people I didn't know, or the ones who didn't live in my small town of Maxwell.

In my heart I knew it would be a mistake, but I also knew the effort wouldn't be wasted. Someone else would buy it at one of the festivals I would attend at a future date.

My angels were my creation, from the idea of the design to the finished product. The thought of doing angels of many different designs came to me when I was sitting in waiting rooms, emergency rooms, and patient rooms in different hospitals in the region where I lived.

All of that hospital attendance was brought on by my husband's many illnesses, most of them being life or death events.

I needed to keep my mind busy, and not dwell on the thought that my husband might actually die.

He suffered for many years with a back problem that required three different surgeries, a heart problem that necessitated a triple bypass and twenty six stents over a fifteen-year period, and diabetes that we both watched diligently. Eventually his heart stopped, and my hospital life came to a halt.

As I sat in the emergency, waiting, and patient rooms, I would keep my sanity by crocheting. I always had my tote bag with me, and I kept it filled with yarn, crochet hooks, and a pattern I had created.

Life went on, and I had to adapt. I knew people would look at me strangely if I told them I missed my hospital sitting time. Of course, they didn't realize it was my husband I was missing, not the hospital.

Onward and upward became my motto as I traveled through one day after another, on my own, without my husband.

CHAPTER 2
MY ANGELS LED ME

My angels led me to new places, where I met new people and enjoyed almost every minute of my new life.

Selling my angels was difficult during the summer months. Most customers would rather not think about the ravages of winter and needing a blanket for warmth.

I branched out into other crocheted items to fill that void. My crocheted baby items, toys, caps, and frilly scarves became my money makers.

I took orders for baby items willingly, but for the angel afghans, I was reluctant. Many times when I completed the angel, the person who placed the order no longer wanted it. My angel did not get her promised home, and had to be placed in a pile to wait for another kind-hearted soul to be willing to let the angel guard his or her life.

I was at the Better Living Show at the Brushfork Armory, in Bluefield, West Virginia. I always considered that specific date, the last weekend in April, as the beginning of my new selling season.

I had worked all winter long, making new items to show and sell. When I was at shows and there was a lull in customer traffic, I could be seen rapidly working at creating stitches for a new angel.

I was tired of the winter season, even though I had looked forward to the downtime at the end of December.

Living alone was wearing heavily on me through the winter months. The onslaught of snow and ice made it almost impossible for me to get out and about to enjoy my friends, with their wonderful conversations.

I held my crocheting in my lap, hook poised for action. I watched the people milling around, taking advantage of the handcrafted items for sale on the mezzanine of the armory.

The person in charge of this event always put crafters on the second level, in a ten-square-foot booth for a much more reasonable price for the two-day event.

I believe I was the only one who was totally alone. I had no family members I could call on to help me man the booth. My two sons worked, and their wives were also busy with trying to make a living.

The one I missed the most was my husband, who would have been right there with me every time his health permitted.

Onward and upward, and away from thoughts that made me sad.

CHAPTER 3
ON THE ROAD AGAIN

It was Friday, the first day of the two-day show. I watched the front door open, allowing the visitors inside the armory. There had been a line of people standing outside, so I had high hopes of selling an angel or two. If not an angel, then maybe they would buy one of the smaller crocheted items I had made for those with less money to spend.

"Betty, how have you been?" I asked the lady who was set up in the booth next to me. She came here to sell her beaded jewelry.

"Great, Molly, and you?" she responded with a smile.

"Just fine. I'm glad to be back on the road again. I was really tired of staying home so much," I answered.

"Me, too. Home and hearth gets a little boring at times, doesn't it?" Betty added.

"I know what you mean," I answered softly. Betty was talking with a possible customer.

I stood behind my table and plastered a smile to my lips, so as not to discourage a possible customer.

Most of the other vendors I could see were sitting. They didn't appear to be happy to see a possible sale.

I always thought it was wonderful to talk to new, interesting people and the smile helped start a conversation, along with the "Hi, how are you?" I said to most everyone who started to walk past my booth.

It took a few minutes for the customers to enter through the front door, work their way between the winding rows of first floor where the big money vendors were on display, and finally climb the steps to the second floor. Customers then had to walk through the rafters to meet and greet us, the crafters.

The booths on the mezzanine were placed in the shape of a U. There were two long sides and one short side, opposite the stage located on the first floor. My booth was in the center of the short side, so I had what I thought was a really good location.

If I walked across the aisle in front of my booth, I could look over the railing to see the entire first floor, except for anyone directly below the overhanging mezzanine.

The customer who had been talking with Betty left without stopping to see my items, so I walked across the aisle to see the people on the first floor moving from booth to booth, collecting all of the freebies and placing them in their shopping bags. To be truthful, that was the reason most of these people attended the show. They wanted the free items.

I always had peppermint puffs on my table. Sometimes it was a challenge to keep up with refilling the basket. I frowned when they took the candies by the handfuls, but that didn't seem to stop them. Not all of them grabbed a handful, but some did take advantage.

I watched a group of elderly people. I knew they would not be able to climb up the steps to our lofty heights.

I also watched a younger man, maybe in his late twenties, following along behind the five or six older folks.

The younger man followed close enough to the elderly group to make it appear he was with them, perhaps as a chaperone.

He appeared to be a clean-cut, young man. He had neatly trimmed hair and a clean-shaven face.

His jerky actions let me know that he was nervous and not accustomed to performing the task at hand, whatever that was.

Because there was no customer activity around my booth at that moment, I continued to watch the young man. I wanted to see what he was planning to do. I had no doubt it would involve the elderly people.

The young man glanced around to see if anyone was watching him. I felt sure he could feel my eyes resting on him, watching his every move. He just had no idea where the watching eyes were located.

There were cameras strategically placed throughout the first floor, but he seemed to know where they were. He would duck his head to hide his face from the camera each time he passed in front of one.

He continued to follow the elderly people, and I continued to watch.

He looked up towards me just as he gently bumped the elderly gentleman walking in front of him.

I saw the young man's hand reach into the back pocket of the white-haired gentleman's pants. He quickly extracted the older man's wallet and snatched his hand back from sight.

When the young man realized I was a witness to the whole scenario, he stopped abruptly and reached to the floor, making it appear that he had found the older man's wallet after it dropped to the floor.

The older man thanked the young man for picking up the dropped wallet, then he shuffled along to catch up with the rest of the group. A grateful smile beamed across his age-lined face.

The young man looked up at me and saluted before rapidly walking away, out of sight.

I smiled to myself and walked back to my booth.

"I guess those angels have been a good influence on me," I mumbled.

"Hi, how are you?" I said, greeting some people approaching my booth.

It felt strange to be an angel on high. I really wasn't an angel; far from it. All I did was prevent a thief from victimizing an elderly man.

I felt good about the whole idea of doing a good deed.

Maybe my angels were guiding me onward and upward, after all.

CHAPTER 4
I GLANCED SKYWARD

"Hi, Abby," I said to the elderly lady setting up beside my booth on the right. Betty was still on my left.

"Molly, how are you?" Abby asked me.

"Fine, but you look a little bit under the weather," I said with concern.

"It was hard bringing these totes up here. It wears me out every time when I have to carry heavy boxes filled with my handmade items up the steps," Abby said softly. She sounded like she was almost out of breath.

"You should have brought everything before four o'clock yesterday afternoon. All those college boys would have brought everything up here for you," I said.

"I forgot," replied Abby.

"In that case, you should have called me. I would have helped. You have my cell phone number, don't you?" I asked.

"Yes, but I didn't want to be a bother," she replied.

I didn't say anything else. That was her usual response.

Abby went about her business of setting up her display.

I helped her any way I could, so we would both be prepared for what we hoped would be an onslaught of customers.

Abby was a seamstress, of sorts. She didn't make fancy items. Oh, they looked good enough, but they were practical and useful. I believe I have at least one of everything she makes, from quilted pot holders to baked potato pockets.

Abby was right about the totes being too heavy for her to carry. She was pushing seventy years old, so anything over ten pounds was a task for her.

"Abby, what's next for you?" I asked, in an effort to fill the void of not talking to a prospective customer.

"I don't have my calendar with me, but I don't think I have anything until next month. I have some family coming in for an extended visit, so I didn't want to commit myself and then have to cancel at the last minute," she explained.

"That's a nice reason to have for not setting up. I can't use that one, due to lack of family members," I said sadly. I needed to change the topic of conversation immediately, or I would fall down the rabbit hole of depression again.

"Molly, have you been to the arts center lately?" asked Abby.

"No, what's going on there?" I asked, grateful for the subject change.

"There's a new director. Well, she's not really new. She was there a few years ago. Her name is Susan Roberts. Do you remember her?" Abby asked.

"Yes, but I didn't care too much about her when she was there the first time," I answered.

"Why didn't you like her?" Abby asked.

"She seems to be a bit of a snob. I hope she's changed, but I rather doubt it. Once a snob, always a snob," I said, as I laughed with the last statement.

"She didn't seem like a snob to me," said Abby.

"Maybe I was having a bad day," I answered. It occurred to me that Abby couldn't see Susan as a snob because they were quite a bit alike. The only real difference between the two of them was about forty years. I could overlook it in Abby, but I couldn't with Susan. She hadn't earned the right to be a snob.

The afternoon was full of activity, with people stopping to talk and make purchases from both of us.

At the end of the selling day, I helped Abby pack up and carry her totes and boxes to her car. Then I carried all of my totes and bags to my car.

My good deed for the day was to help Abby. She really needed it, because she was so very tired. Age was creeping up on her, and I could see that clearly written on her face.

Before I left the armory, I glanced skyward to see if I could find any angels hovering over the place. I thought maybe they might have been the reason Abby and I both sold merchandise as well as we did.

"Onward and upward," I whispered as I drove away for the day.

CHAPTER 5
I'M NO GOODY TWO-SHOES

I was sitting around the house being bored. I don't like being bored. Boredom sometimes leads me into depression, and I wanted to stay out of that deep, dark rabbit hole.

"I'm going to do it," I mumbled. I hunted for my phone book to look up the number for the Maxwell Community Hospital.

"Maxwell Community Hospital, how can I direct you?" said a perky, cheerful voice.

"Volunteer Office, please," I answered.

"Volunteer Office, Martha speaking," said an older, not so perky voice.

"What do I have to do to become a volunteer in the gift shop?" I asked.

"You need to fill out an application first, then you will receive a call from one of us telling you when to come in to be trained. That's all. With whom am I speaking?" she asked in a friendly tone.

"My name is Molly Thompson. My husband spent many days and nights in your hospital at many different times, and all of your wonderful doctors and nurses saved his life each of those times. He had a really bad heart condition, you know. Well, anyway, I decided it was time I did something for the hospital. It won't be much, but I want to do what I can," I explained.

"That's wonderful, Molly. I think I remember seeing you during those trying times," Martha said.

"Yeah, well, he passed away about six years ago, and I've finally retired from work so now I can work for you," I continued.

"I'm sorry to hear about your husband's passing, but I'm sure you would be welcomed into the auxiliary to help us out from time to time. I just need your address, and I will mail the application to you right away. We can surely use your help," said Martha with a little more cheer in her voice.

"Thank you," I said. I replaced the phone receiver into its cradle after reciting my address.

I am no goody two-shoes, but I want to help when I can. Money was a scarce commodity in my household, but time was something I was willing to donate.

It was like the work I did for the local county fair. It only happened one week out of the year, but I gave them as much time as I possibly could. I had been a willing volunteer for the county fair for about twenty years. I always thought the county fair was the best yearly event in Maxwell County, and I wanted to see it stay around forever.

During the first week of August, excitement filled the air and anticipation would build until I saw the rides with lights shining bright against the black night sky. All of the rides were adorned with many bright bulbs that would entice everyone to enter the fairyland of the traveling carnival.

I was one of those people who stood at the front gate, rain or shine, and collected tickets or money for admittance into the grounds for fun, games, and rides.

It was hard, at times. That was usually weather related, but I didn't complain. I needed to do something to thank those people for entertaining the folks of Maxwell County with a fair.

I wanted to continue working at the fair, but I needed to do something else. Volunteering at the hospital one half-day a week would help me fill the need. It would help me move onward and upward.

CHAPTER 6
TRAINING DAY

I was all excited about my new opportunity to make new friends, and fill my lonely hours with an activity that would keep me away from home and the memories that replayed in my mind.

It wasn't that I ever wanted to forget about my Tommy, but I did want to move on and not live in my mind all the time. Life goes on for everyone, and that included me.

I dressed in office-type clothes for training. I wanted to be presentable and professional in the gift shop.

The person who was my teacher for training day was Linda Mason. She was a tall, slender woman, with brown hair mixed with streaks of gray. She wore silver, wire-rimmed glasses and spoke with a soft-sounding authority.

She led me through the opening routine first, followed by the closing routine so that I would know what to do at the end of the day, just in case.

Because there were two of us working on training day, I thought I would always have a work partner. Well, I was wrong. When I received my permanent assignment, it was every Wednesday morning, and I would be working alone.

That was not what I wanted. I wanted to make a few friends. Working alone every Wednesday wasn't going to allow me to do that.

Wednesday rolled around and I went to the hospital gift shop early so I could open up, count the money supplied for change, and generally look at what was available for sale to the public and employees.

I brought a couple of magazines with me to read.

"Molly, how are you doing?" asked Nancy, the admission clerk from across the hall.

"Just fine. How are you doing, Nancy?" I said cheerfully, grateful for someone with whom I could talk.

"Okay. It's a little slow this morning. I guess that's a good thing. People aren't sick enough to visit the emergency room," she said, with a shrug of her shoulders.

"I suppose so," I agreed.

"Look out the window, Molly. I think there might be a little business coming our way right now," Nancy said as she pointed out the window to the flashing lights of the police car that was parking outside.

"What's happening?" I asked.

"I don't know, but I'll go see," Nancy said, as she left the gift shop.

I stood next to the window, watching the Maxwell police officer open the back door of the vehicle to remove a prisoner from the back seat. The man had his hands cuffed behind his back, but he was leaning over to accommodate some kind of pain. His pain was evident in his face, and the grimace contorted his features.

The police officer wasn't displaying a lot of sympathy. He had his gun drawn, at the ready, as he pushed the prisoner forward.

"Must be a really, really bad guy," I mumbled. I watched until the two of them disappeared through the automatic doors.

I returned to the desk behind the counter and started paging through my magazine.

My eyes were getting heavy. Absolutely no one had entered the gift shop for about an hour.

An alarm began to blare, the lights flashed, and a security guard appeared in the doorway.

"What's going on?" I asked as I shook the sleepiness from my brain by shaking my head from side to side.

"A prisoner has escaped. I was sent here to lock you inside until the all-clear sounds," he explained.

I grabbed the door key and ran to the door.

"Don't you need to leave?" I asked excitedly.

"No, ma'am. I was told to stay with you," he said calmly.

"Why?" I asked.

"They think the prisoner might rob you to get some spending money," he explained.

"Oh, I guess this is one of the few places with cash money. I don't have very much in the register. I haven't had any customers this morning," I said slowly.

My mind was telling me there was something wrong with this picture.

I grabbed the front door key and turned the lock from the inside. I returned to the counter, where I pulled out a chair for the security guard to use.

"Take a load off," I instructed the security guard as I forced a broad smile to my aging face.

"I'll just stand, ma'am. I need to keep an eye out on what's going on," he answered nervously.

"Well, I'll leave it there just in case," I said. My smile disappeared.

I started paging through my magazine as I sneaked peeks at the security guard. He was sweating, and he wiped his face against the sleeve of his upraised arm.

"It's getting hot in here. I can see why you leave the door open all the time," he said as he glanced at me.

"It's a little warm," I said. I pulled my jacket closed. Actually I was a bit chilly, but I didn't want to tell him that, not yet anyway.

The security guard walked to the front windows, which faced the patient pick-up area in the center of the little drive around. Then he turned and crossed the small room to look out the window facing the lobby's waiting area. He kept up that back and forth pacing and looking for a few minutes, getting more nervous with each glance out of the window.

"John, you might as well have a seat. There is nothing moving around anywhere," I said.

He glanced down at his shirt, read the name printed on the removable name tag and said, "My name is Dan, not John."

"I'm sorry. I thought I saw John," I added.

Perspiration beaded up across his nose and started dripping off the tip. He was way too nervous to be a security guard.

He wiped his face with his sleeve again, then placed his hand on the gun at his side. He didn't remove it from its holster, but he did release the small strap that had been holding it in place.

Now I was getting nervous. Like I said, there was something wrong with this picture.

I slowly opened a drawer of the desk and started feeling around inside, searching for a defensive weapon of some sort.

Nothing.

I slid the drawer closed and pulled open the next one down.

"What are you doing?" the security guard snarled.

"Nothing. Just checking out what's in the drawers. I don't work every day, so I check it out once in a while. It's hard to tell what the other ladies have stuffed in here," I said as I tried to smile.

"Stop it. You're making me nervous," he snapped.

"Okay," I snapped back at him. I noisily slid the second drawer closed while I pulled on the third one. I leaned forward to hide the fact that I had opened the bottom drawer.

"How long have you worked here, Dan?" I asked. I leaned my chin onto my right palm, which I had propped up against the desk.

"Why?" he demanded.

"Just wondering. I just started here today myself, so I don't know very many of the employees," I answered in a conversational tone.

"Is that right?" asked the security guard.

"Yes, it's my solo debut," I said with a forced smile.

"I guess you picked the wrong day to start working here," he added sarcastically. "You're a volunteer, aren't you?"

"Yes, I am finally past sixty-five so I could retire from my job at the school board office. I needed something to do to fill my time after my husband died," I explained. I was hoping my age and gray hair would serve as a deterrent to violence on his part.

I glanced down at the opened drawer and saw a strange-looking leather apparatus. I wanted to pick it up and take a closer look, but I knew that was out of the question.

"Get over here," the security guard whispered harshly.

"Why?" I asked, as I stood up from my chair.

"Don't ask why. Just get over here," he snarled.

"Wait a second. I need to put my shoe back on my foot," I said. I bent over to grab the weighted leather strap. I held the strap-filled hand behind my back as I scooted out from behind the counter.

"Get over here with the key and stand right here," he said as he pointed to the area in front of the door.

"Are you leaving?" I asked.

"Yeah," he said as he watched me.

I had the key in one hand and the weighted leather strap in the other. I continued to hide the leather strap as I tried with one hand to adjust the key to the proper grip. When I got close to the door, I allowed the key to slip from my grip.

"Oops!" I said. The key clattered to the floor.

The security guard watched me as he reached for the fallen key. When his head went down, my arm went up, so I could build speed and momentum to crash the weighted strap down against his head. I hit him with all of the strength I could muster. With the weighted end of the leather strap, it knocked him to the floor, lights out.

I ran around the counter and reached for the gift shop phone, after I picked up his gun from the floor.

I dialed the operator and said, "I need help. Send the police to the gift shop. Someone was in here holding a gun on me," I said excitedly. Then I hung up the receiver so I could watch his every move.

I walked back to the door, located the key on the floor, and placed it in the lock. I turned the lock and waited.

Two uniformed town police officers came around the corner with guns drawn.

"Open the door, ma'am," shouted one of the officers.

"I can't. He's right in front of it," I explained.

One of the officers walked up to the door and pulled at the door. He opened it slowly, as the second officer held a gun pointed at the man on the floor.

"What did you do to him?" asked the first officer as he cuffed the unconscious man.

I held up the weighted leather strap and said, "I hit him over the head with this. You can have the strap and his gun. Take them, please."

"You must have had an angel on your shoulder, ma'am," said the second officer.

"Why would you say that?" I asked.

"This man killed two people in the emergency room. He could have killed you," the officer answered.

"You'll need to come down to the police station and make a statement as to what has happened here," said the first officer.

"Yes, sir. I'll lock up here and meet you there," I said in a shaky voice.

I heard them instruct some late-arriving officers to put up some tape, so the detectives could check everything out when they arrived.

I locked the door and walked to the reception window, where I handed the girl the key to the gift shop.

"The detectives or town police officers will need to investigate," I said softly. "Give them the key when they get here. I'm leaving."

I sat in my car in the parking lot and tried to stop my shaking body from moving. Once the shaking stopped, the tears started.

I cried for a while.

I thought about what could have happened, and what actually did happen.

I cried some more.

I guessed that maybe I did have an angel on my shoulder, and I was ever so grateful. I looked upward in my effort to move onward.

CHAPTER 7
THE FLASH

I drove to the police station, where I wrote out my statement about what had happened. The officers were very nice to me, but they wanted every meticulous detail.

This was not the first time I'd had a confrontation that required a legal investigation.

My thoughts went back to when my Tommy was alive.

***

"Tommy, what are you doing?" I asked. I watched his hand slide over to pull on the lever attached to the steering column of our car.

"I'm just being courteous," he responded with a smile. "That big old eighteen wheeler is trying to get over in our lane in front of me, and I'm letting him know it's okay."

"You know that driver will come on over without the flashing headlights, don't you?" I questioned him. I tried to understand why he insisted on being kind to the drivers who would force their will onto him anyway.

"Yeah, I know, but it doesn't hurt to be nice sometimes, you know."

"I guess not," was my only response. No use arguing. He was going to do it anyway, no matter what I said.

It was going to be a long drive.

Tommy had an appointment at the Veterans Administration Clinic, about ninety miles from home. Why they couldn't schedule him an appointment at a health facility closer to our house was truly beyond my comprehension. I knew for a fact that a friend of mine had a husband who saw a local doctor, and everything was charged to the Veterans Administration.

We decided to suck it up and not make waves. It took forever and a day to get the Veterans Administration to pay for any part of his health care. I was afraid they would take it away completely, if we fussed about the drive.

Tommy had so many health problems that I needed all the help I could get from anywhere I could get it, and that included the small portion that the Veterans Administration paid.

"How are you feeling, Tommy?" I asked this question at least ten times a day.

"I'm all right, I just have a twinge in my back."

"Do you want me to drive?" I asked, knowing what his answer would be.

"No, I can make it all right. I know how you hate to drive," he said as he tried to make me feel guilty. Or maybe make me feel better, I wasn't sure.

Again, I saw him flash his lights to allow a truck driver access to the driving space in front of our vehicle.

I didn't say anything. What was the use?

The appointment was short and sweet, but too late in the day for my liking. I believed its only purpose was to make sure the Veterans Administration patient was still alive and kicking, and was authorized to receive his medications through the mail until the summons to appear at the clinic arose again.

Of course by the time we departed for home and hearth, the hour was late and darkness was falling upon our part of the world.

Tommy was a good, kind soul who liked to watch out for the other guy.

"Look at that man over there. He doesn't even have his headlights turned on. He's going to get himself killed," he said. He pulled the lever again to flash our car headlights, as a warning or signal to force the oncoming driver to take notice and turn on his headlights.

"Tommy, you don't need to take care of the world. Maybe you shouldn't be doing that," I said. I watched the headlight-less driver pass us slowly and cautiously, as though he were trying to memorize everything about us.

"Well, Molly, I would want someone to let me know if I didn't have my headlights shining brightly at night."

I was uncomfortable about the flashing headlights. I couldn't put my finger on a real reason for the feeling.

I guessed this feeling thing went back to my youth, when I realized that I might have some psychic abilities. After I realized that my feelings were predictors of doom and destruction, I made myself get over it. I willed myself to not be able to predict the future actions of family and friends. I wanted to know nothing about the future or the outcome of my many mistakes. Until now.

That black cloud was hovering over me, over this car, and I didn't know what to do about it.

Why did I turn away from knowing the future?

We lived in a rural area of southwest Virginia. So it wasn't unusual for the interstate to be deserted as soon as the sun dropped below the horizon. It was as if there was a curfew that covered all of Maxwell County.

"Tommy, are you okay?" I asked again softly. I didn't want to sound critical in any way.

"Yeah, but that car that I flashed my lights at a few minutes ago is following us. I wonder what this is all about," he said as he cast a nervous glance at his rearview mirror.

I wanted to tell him "I told you so," but I forced my mouth to stay tightly closed.

I turned around in my seat and looked out the back window.

"He is awfully close. Speed up a little."

"All right, but I don't want to get a ticket."

"There isn't a cop out around here for miles. Just speed up. I don't know what kind of game this guy is playing, but I don't like it one little bit."

He tromped on the gas pedal and I felt the car jerk forward.

Suddenly, I felt a different kind of movement with the car.

"He's pushing us, Tommy!"

"I know, I know. I'm trying to keep the car on the road. If I press on the brake, he might force us to slide over the bank."

Tommy was struggling with the steering wheel. The car was weaving dangerously back and forth across two lanes. He kept turning the wheel toward the center line so that we wouldn't jump the guard rail and fly down the mountainside.

"Lights ahead, Tommy! I think he might back off a little until that oncoming car gets past us. I hope that's what he will do. Maybe we can get a little bit ahead of him. Maybe we can get far enough ahead that we can turn off onto another road and lose that crazy man," I said, nervously rattling on. I was unable to stop myself from talking.

"Just shut up for a minute, Molly! Let me think, okay?" he shouted angrily. His knuckles turned white because he was clutching the steering wheel so tightly.

"Are you okay?" I asked as I remembered his heart condition. This excitement and fear could very easily lead the way to another heart attack.

"Do I look okay?" he snapped. "Even if I weren't, what could you do about it?"

I was too scared to be angry with him.

The car wasn't being pushed anymore. The idiot behind us must have seen the oncoming headlights, too.

"Step on it, Tommy. Maybe we can get away from this crazy guy," I screamed at him so he could see my panic.

Tommy's face was a stone mask of determination and grit as he gripped the steering wheel with all of his might. He stepped on the gas pedal, flooring it to accelerate into a speed zone beyond my imagination.

I turned to face the rear window and saw that the monster was growing smaller and smaller in the distance.

"Is there some place ahead where you can turn, without him seeing you?"

"Maybe. If I can get to a curve where the bend keeps him from spotting us make the turn, maybe I can lose him."

I kept my head turned to the rear so I could tell if and when he'd lost sight of us.

"Now, Tommy, I can't see him now!" I screamed excitedly.

"There's no place to turn. Wait—keep watching. Up ahead, there is a road to the left up ahead. Maybe I can turn off there. Then turn off to hide somewhere. God, I hope this works," he said. He turned the wheel to the left, lifting the passenger side wheels off the ground. He had extinguished the headlights on our car, but thankfully, there was a little bit of daylight left. It was just enough for us to see the road ahead.

"Dear, God, help us," I prayed, as the tires on my side of the car gripped pavement again.

"Hang on, I'm making a whop-dam-dilly of a turn right now."

The car turned to the right as fiercely as it had previously turned to the left. I was thrown against the passenger side door so hard that I feared it would burst open from the pressure of my overweight body hitting against it. I didn't want to think about the marks that would become apparent where my flesh and door collided.

Then we weren't moving at all.

The car came to a complete stop.

When I collected enough of my wits about me to look towards Tommy, I realized he had shut off the engine and was breathing heavily, with loud rasping breaths.

"Tommy, what's wrong?" I asked.

"I'm just trying to catch my breath, that's all," he said breathlessly.

"Is your chest hurting?" I asked.

"A little, but I'm too revved up to let it kick in too much. I really don't want to think about my heart. Not now anyway," he said. His breathing gradually became slower, with normal intakes and exhales. Finally, I focused on the world outside of the car.

We were behind a building of some kind, beneath some low hanging branches that partially blocked the view from the road. Our car was neutral beige and blended in with the background of darkness and tree branches.

"How did you know about this place?" I whispered, as if I thought someone other than Tommy could hear me.

"I didn't. I just took a chance," he said calmly.

"How long do you think we'll have to wait before we can go home?" I asked.

"Your guess is as good as mine," he answered.

I found myself holding my breath, as if I were afraid that the maniac chasing us would hear me breathe.

Tommy's breathing had calmed and he was almost back to normal.

We sat in that car, motionless, waiting for the monster car to come crashing into us.

The seconds ticked by in slow motion. The minutes seemed like hours. The waiting was horrible.

My mind was wearing itself out, picturing scenarios of what might happen if the driver of the monster car found us.

I glanced at my watch.

"It's been over an hour. What do you think, Tommy?" I asked impatiently.

"I'm tired of waiting. Let's make a break for it," he said, trying to throw some humor into our situation.

He started the car, shifted it into drive, and we hurried out of our hiding spot.

I was all eyeballs as I tried to look into every nook and cranny we passed along each side of the road. My eyes grew tired of wide-eyed staring, so I refrained from trying to see the whole world as it passed us by, along both sides of the road.

"I haven't seen any sign of him, Tommy. Do you think he went on his merry way?" I asked.

"I hope so, Molly," he said. I saw him relax a little, loosening up the muscles in his hands and wrists by releasing his grip on the steering wheel to the point that he was only touching it softly, almost caressing it.

I tried to relax, but I couldn't. I felt the presence of the black cloud scudding through the sky, hanging above us, reminding me that it wasn't over yet. It wouldn't be over until we were safely at home with the doors locked and the shades drawn, allowing us to stay hidden in our own little cozy world.

My wide-eyed watching didn't let me scope out the entire surroundings in one big view. Instead, I slowly glanced from one side of the road to the other. I wanted to be able to catch any kind of movement, no matter how insignificant it was.

"Tommy, is that a car pulled over to the side, under that bridge? I suppose he's playing hide and seek now."

"Yeah, I think it is him. I need to get closer to tell for sure. I think he's playing a killing game, and we're it," he said sarcastically.

"If it isn't him, that's not a very safe place to be broken down. Of course, there is no safe place to be broken down, is there?" I asked, rattling on nervously.

"It looks like his car, Molly. I think he's hiding there, waiting for us to drive by so he can chase us again," he said angrily.

"Why?" I whispered softly. I saw his hands and wrists assume their previous tense positions.

"I don't know. I really don't have any idea, Molly," he said loudly.

"Is there any place we can go? Do we have to drive past that maniac?" I asked.

"No, there's no place to turn. We have to keep driving, no matter what happens," he said, as calmly as he could.

Tommy speeded the car up and raced past the car, which looked dark and empty.

I looked back and saw bright headlights come to life. The car pulled onto the road and raced to catch up with us.

"He must have been scrunched down in the seat, Tommy! He's coming after us!" I screamed. I saw the gap between the cars shrinking.

Tommy was an excellent driver, but he had a chronic heart condition that could make itself known in a flash. *How could his heart, working at a level only twenty-five percent of a normal heart, stand the stress, fear, and fatigue this stupid car chase could be causing?*

"Are you all right, Tommy?" I asked again.

He didn't answer me. He was concentrating solely on how we were going to get out of this mess.

Tommy glanced at the rearview mirror, and I turned my body to face the rear. I removed my seat belt because I needed the freedom to turn my body more than the constricting belt would allow.

I was having trouble seeing our chaser, but he was there. He had turned off his headlights so we'd have a much harder time spotting him, and gauging his distance. He was right about that. The darkness of the night and the absence of the headlights forced me to strain my eyes and gaze into what appeared to be black emptiness, once I searched beyond the area of our own vehicle lights.

"Molly, keep watch for me. I can't tell how close he is," Tommy instructed.

"I'll do the best I can. I can't see very much, either. I wish it were a cloudless night. The clouds are only making it darker and harder to see," I said in response.

"How am I doing? Am I staying ahead of him?" shouted Tommy.

"I think so," I replied.

24

"I see some lights from traffic ahead. That will help, I hope. If we get into some traffic, we might be able to lose him," he said excitedly.

I continued to watch out the rear window, searching for the next onslaught of speed coming toward us.

Tommy worked the car into the middle of the traffic pod so that we could find protection in numbers. He maintained only the speed necessary to stay with the traffic, and we both prayed that the group of cars would not break up and scatter. That would be an open invitation for our pursuer to continue his game.

We finally arrived at our exit from the interstate, and I hoped beyond all hopes that some of the traffic pod would exit with us.

All of the vehicles except one began cruising down the exit, much to our happy surprise. We stayed with the crowd until we arrived at the Maxwell Police Station, where we turned into the parking lot and quickly exited the car. We walked in through the front door to report our problem.

"Brian Harris? Is he here? We really need to speak to Brian Harris," I sputtered breathlessly.

"Yes, ma'am, I'll go see if he is busy. What is your name?" asked a young man dressed as a uniformed police officer.

"Thompson, Molly, and my husband is Tommy Thompson. He knows me from the school board office. I used to work there," I explained.

The deputy behind the long counter walked toward an office in the rear of the room. After a few moments, he returned to say, "Chief Harris will be with you in a moment."

"Hey, Molly, how are you doing?" asked a cheerful Police Chief Brian Harris.

"Not so good, Brian, or should I call you Chief?"

"Brian is fine. What's wrong?"

"Tommy and I were being chased on the interstate by some kind of nut, the crazy kind, if you know what I mean. His game was to run us off the road. I really think he was trying to actually kill us," I said in a voice that kept rising in volume, due to my fear and dread.

"Did you see the guy?" asked Brian.

"Only a glimpse, I never saw him before today. How about you, Tommy? Have you seen this guy before?" I asked.

"No, I can't say that I have," Tommy answered.

25

Then I went on to explain how we tried to outrun him, until we finally turned off the road and hid from sight. I continued with the revelation that he was waiting under the bridge for us to pass by, so he could continue his pursuit.

"The only way we were able to lose him was to get into the middle of a group of cars and stay there until we reached our exit," I said.

"Did he follow you off the exit?" asked Brian.

"Yes, actually he was behind us when we turned into your parking lot. He might still be waiting for us outside," I said as I glanced toward the window.

"What kind of car was it?" asked Brian.

"An SUV, one of the smaller ones. I really don't know all the makes and models. It was dark green, I think. It was dark and we can only guess at the color," I said.

"Did you get a license plate number?" asked Brian.

"No, my eyesight isn't too good and it's even worse at night. It seemed like it was covered with dirt or mud, so I couldn't make out the numbers. I couldn't even tell you if it was a Virginia plate or not," I explained.

"You didn't cut him off or anything like that to cause what they call road rage, did you?" asked Brian, glancing at me with raised eyebrows.

"No, actually Tommy was trying to be nice. He flashed his lights when he saw the other driver's headlights weren't on. It's a courtesy flash that should be helpful, not hurtful," I said.

"Would you guys excuse me for a minute? I need to check something out," said Brian. He left the room.

Brian returned with a piece of paper clutched in his hand.

"Molly, you and Tommy need to read this," he said. He thrust the paper toward me. "This just came in over the Internet."

State Police Warning (Serious)

DON'T FLASH HEADLIGHTS AT ANY CAR WITH NO LIGHTS ON!!

Police officers working with the DARE program have issued this warning:

If you are driving after dark and see an oncoming car with no headlights on, DO NOT FLASH YOUR LIGHTS AT THEM! This is a common Hellhounds member 'initiation game' that goes like this:

The new gang member under initiation drives along with no headlights, and the first car to flash their headlights at him is now his 'target.'

He is now required to turn around and chase that car, then shoot and kill every individual in the vehicle in order to complete his initiation requirements. Police departments across the nation are being warned.

Their intent is to have all the new Hellhounds nationwide drive around on Friday and Saturday nights with their headlights off. In order to be accepted into the gang, they have to shoot and kill all individuals in the first auto that does a courtesy flash to warn them that their lights are off. Make sure you share this information with all the drivers in your family!

Please forward this message to all your friends and family members to inform them about the initiation ritual.

Signed/Dispatcher/Kentucky State Police

"Is this for real?" I asked Brian in disbelief. I handed the paper to Tommy so he could read it.

"I don't know, but it sounds like that initiation game and it is happening to you," said Brian.

"What can we do?" I asked apprehensively.

"I guess we have to catch him in the act," added Brian.

"In the act of what, killing us?" I asked in a high-pitched voice teetering on the verge of a scream.

"Well, yes. We really need to catch him stalking you, chasing you, with the intent to do you harm," said Brian.

"You're kidding. Tommy's heart can't stand all that kind of stress. He has a bad heart, it's been keeping us running to Roanoke every month. I can't take that kind of chance with his life," I said, a little louder than necessary.

"Okay. Tommy can stay here at the police station. I'll leave with you, Molly, and I will be wearing Tommy's jacket and hat. We'll convince the man chasing you that I'm Tommy," said Brian.

"Sounds scary, maybe too scary for me," I said. I tried to absorb what Brian was telling me.

27

"Oh, it's scary, all right. But when you and your husband leave this building, he could be waiting for you around the corner. That's what I hope he's doing, so I can catch him. But he's going to have to believe I'm Tommy. If you and Tommy leave here, you might not make it to your house. Do you understand, Molly? Tommy?" asked Brian.

Both Tommy and I nodded our heads up and down, like school children who were being scolded.

"When do you want to do this?" I asked, hoping the answer would be "never."

"I'll check with my officers who are here, right now. I will need some back up, so I need to get everyone here involved. You guys just sit tight for a few minutes. I'll be right back with you."

"What do you think, Tommy?" I asked.

"I really don't want you to do this," he answered.

"I don't think I have a choice," I said.

"Neither do I," he said. He rubbed his chest.

"Are you hurting?" I asked, with worry in my tone.

"Yeah, a little," said Tommy.

"On a scale of one to ten, what is it?" I asked.

"About a six," he answered.

"That's more than a little," I protested.

"Yeah, I know, but I can't do anything about it right at this moment," Tommy said.

"No, I guess not," I agreed.

"Tommy, if you don't mind lending me your jacket and cap, Molly and I will be on our way to your home. If we don't run into any problems, I'll have an officer drive you home to be with Molly, then I'll go back to the office. If there's a problem, Molly, my officers and I will have to take care of business, and then you can be driven home. How does that sound?' said Brian.

Tommy shrugged his shoulders, but he looked like he was very near tears.

I knew he wanted to participate, and help me to help us. I knew he couldn't, and he knew he couldn't. That didn't make it any easier.

Brian and I walked slowly to the door. My knees were turning to jelly, not wanting to support me. I grabbed hold of the doorknob and tried to hide my fear.

Brian hunched his shoulders a bit, trying to convince any onlookers that his middle-aged frame was one of a man in his sixties.

I didn't have to pretend at anything. I was a fifty-nine year old woman who was absolutely scared to put one foot in front of the other.

"Are you all right, Molly?" whispered Brian. He held the car door open for me, so that I could climb in and continue this charade.

"No, not really, but I'll manage," I answered. My words were different from my normal response of "I will survive." I was not sure of the survival part.

Brian slowly walked around the car, holding onto it for support just like Tommy would. He climbed in, fastened his seat belt, and after shifting into drive, headed for my house.

We knew that if the stalker was waiting for us, he would be just out of sight of the Police Station because we were on a one-way street. We had no choice but to pass him. All he had to do was be patient and wait for us.

Again, I was wide-eyed and scared. I knew my life was going to end just a few feet ahead. All that was missing to make this picture complete, the one that was forming in my brain, was the dark green SUV.

"There, there, over there pulled into that parking lot, facing out to the street, that's him!" I shouted. I pointed towards the direction of the parked car.

"We'll slow down a little, so he can get a good look at us. Don't give him the idea that we are looking for him. Don't point at him anymore. Get his license plate number," said Brian slowly and calmly. He tried to get me to lower my pointing finger.

"Oh, okay, I won't point. You did see the SUV, didn't you?" I asked excitedly.

"Yes ma'am, I did," said Brian.

Brian fiddled around in his jacket pocket and pulled out a radio.

"I want you to turn towards me. While I hold the button down, I want you to tell the officers behind us what the license plate number is. You read it, didn't you?" asked Brian.

"Yes sir. It's YMS3304—Virginia plate," I said.

29

"Repeat it again now," urged Brian.

"Virginia plate YMS3304," I repeated.

He released the button.

"Keep facing me like we're having a conversation, Molly. When I press the button again, ask them if they got the number and if they see the vehicle," instructed Brian.

"Did you get the number, and can you see the vehicle?" I asked

The reply was "ten-four."

"How much further is it until we turn onto your street?" asked Brian.

"About a mile further," I answered,

"I'm going to slow down and pull into the parking lot of that grocery store. When I park in one of the slots, I want you to go inside and meet with the officer there, who will be back by the meat counter. Give him your coat, scarf, and handbag after you remove your wallet and identification. He'll walk back out to the car with a bag of groceries to help hide his face, and climb into the car with me. Do you understand what I'm telling you?" asked Brian.

"Yes, but why can't I stay with you?" I asked.

"Like you said before, this is going to get scary," answered Brian.

"Okay, okay, but let me tell them to let my husband know," I pleaded.

"I already did that before we left the building," said Brian.

I walked into the grocery store, fearing that this game was going to get costly. Again, I regretted not reinforcing my psychic abilities from the past,

The manager of the grocery store asked me to step into his office, to remove me from the exposure that might get me and his customers killed. He was not happy about this situation. His nervousness was evident, and he barely spoke to me. When he did speak, he was not pleasant.

I sat in the manager's office for what seemed to be an eternity, feeling unwelcome and worrying about what was happening with my husband, and with the two men pretending to be Tommy and me.

There appeared to be some kind of excitement taking place at the front of the grocery store, so the manager left me sitting in the office while he checked out the commotion.

The voices were getting louder and my curiosity was getting the better of me.

30

I walked to the front of the grocery store, pushing an empty food cart to hide my real reason for being present.

"...a shootout about a mile from here. Two cops are holed up inside a house. Must be some kind of drug bust gone bad. Don't know for sure," shouted an excited voice over the gathering crowd.

I felt my knees weaken and my world started spinning.

"Get a grip," I said to myself, as I tried to stay conscious. *Are Brian and that other officer, the one dressed like me, okay? What happens if he gets away? Will he continue to come after Tommy and me? What are we supposed to do now?*

I reached into my pocket for my cellphone. I needed to call the police station and check on Tommy. I needed to know what was happening. A telephone book, I needed a telephone book.

I left the empty grocery cart standing unattended and ran back to the manager's office, where I grabbed a phone book.

"Maxwell Police Department, the phone number for the Maxwell Police..." I mumbled over and over again, as if that was going to help me find the number faster.

The number rang and rang without an answer.

"What is going on?" I cried into the unanswered receiver.

The ringing continued.

"Hello," said a loud voice.

"Hello, this is Molly Thompson. My husband, Tommy, is in your office. I need to talk with him."

"Mrs. Thompson, you need to come to this office right now," said the voice.

"I can't. Chief Harris has my car. He dropped me off at the grocery store for safekeeping, and he and another officer proceeded to my house, pretending to be me and my husband. I have no way of getting to the police station, short of walking. These tired, nearly sixty-year-old legs will not handle that long walk. What's the problem? Is my husband all right?"

"You need to get here, Mrs. Thompson, right now," urged the voice.

"Can you come and pick me up? I don't have a way there, and your boss has my car," I said worriedly.

"No ma'am, I can't leave. There's too much going on. Your husband isn't feeling well," said the voice.

"Call an ambulance to take him to the emergency room. I'll find a way to the hospital," I instructed.

The grocery store manager finally returned to his office. The commotion seemed to have subsided.

I didn't even know his name. I looked on his shirt, at the name embroidered on a patch above his pocket.

"Jerry, I need a ride to the hospital. Chief Harris has my car, and my husband is being taken to the emergency room right now, in an ambulance. Could you give me a lift? Do you know anyone who could take me there? I'll be glad to pay them a couple of dollars," I said.

"No ma'am, I can't take you. I'll see if the produce manager can give you a lift," he said, and he was gone again.

He came back into the office with a slender, fresh-faced, young man.

"This lady needs a ride to the hospital. Take her, Johnny, her husband is sick," instructed the grocery store manager.

The two of us exited the store from the rear and walked to a banged-up pickup truck, where we climbed aboard for the short trip. Thank goodness he had a step beneath the passenger door of the truck, because my short legs and fat body would not have been able to get into the vehicle without a little help.

As I tried to straighten myself up from my very un-lady-like crawl into the pickup truck, I paused to look at the ambulance traveling by at a high rate of speed. It had sirens blaring and lights flashing to clear the path in front of the driver. It was headed to the hospital from the direction of my house, not from where my husband was. I breathed a sigh of relief, knowing that Tommy was not in the ambulance that was in such a great hurry.

When we pulled out into traffic, another ambulance came up behind us with sirens screaming and lights flashing as it, too headed toward the hospital.

"Johnny, I think we had better stop at the police station first," I said in soft, calm tones to the young man driving the truck. I was having one of those feelings that made me think twice about what I was doing.

He pulled into the parking lot and as I climbed out of the pickup in an ungainly fashion, he told me he would wait until I gave him a signal to leave.

I smiled and thanked him for being so nice.

I entered the police station, and saw my husband slumped over in a chair.

"Tommy, Tommy, are you okay?" I said to him loudly, and a bit too harshly.

He raised his head up, clutching his chest.

I pulled him up from the chair and guided him out to the same pickup truck I had climbed out of a few minutes earlier.

"Johnny, you need to take us to the hospital. I guess we got here before the ambulance," I said. I helped Tommy into the pickup, to sit between Johnny and me.

"Yes ma'am," he said, as he slammed the vehicle into gear.

I crawled out of the truck at the emergency room and rounded up a wheelchair. Johnny helped me get Tommy into the chair, and I pushed him into the waiting area for the doctor.

After one look at Tommy from the emergency room nurse, nothing needed to be said. She pushed his wheelchair into the nearest unoccupied trauma room and helped him onto the cot, reaching for the oxygen to give him some of the extra air he needed.

"This will help. We have two gunshot victims here ahead of you. Are you able to wait a few minutes?" she asked. She glanced at the curtains drawn around the two cubicles where doctors and nurses were fighting to keep both people alive.

Tommy motioned for the nurse to attend to the other emergencies.

We waited.

We had no idea who the gunshot victims were, behind those drawn curtains. I was hoping and praying one of the cubicles held the man who had been trying to kill us.

The second cubicle had to be a law enforcement officer, of that I had no doubt. Did I want the officer to be Chief Harris? Of course not. No way did I want my friend to be downed by a bullet he'd taken for me, or for Tommy. I didn't want any other police officer to fall victim to the same fate. Truthfully, I didn't want anyone hurt; well, maybe the one who caused all of this to happen, maybe he should be hurting a little bit. No way did I want anyone dead or ruined for life.

Then again, both cubicles could contain the bodies of law enforcement officers. The man who had been chasing us could have escaped. *God, I hope not. That would be the worst scenario I could imagine. He would still be chasing Tommy and me to kill us.*

We waited.

Suddenly the curtains were pulled from around one of the cubicles, and the gurney was pushed rapidly from the emergency room through the double doors, into the inner sanctum of the hospital. Nurses and doctors were running alongside the rolling bed, carrying IV bottles and tending to the prone body on the bed.

The hair color, what little I could see of it, told me that it was Chief Harris.

The lone nurse who remained in the emergency room walked toward our cubicle.

"That was Chief Harris, wasn't it?" I said in a loud whisper.

She nodded her head to tell me yes, and proceeded to check on my husband.

"Are you okay, Mr. Thompson?" she asked, wrapping the blood pressure cuff around his arm.

"I'm hurting. Could I get something for pain?" pleaded Tommy.

"I'll check with the doctor as soon as he gets back. How bad is it on the scale?" asked the nurse.

"About an eight, and the pain is not wanting to go away," answered Tommy.

"As soon as the doctor gets back, I'll get the pain medication. I promise, Mr. Thompson," assured the nurse.

Tommy nodded his head and sighed as she walked to the cubicle that had remained curtained.

We waited.

I watched the slow-moving clock. Another hour had passed, and Tommy had not seen the doctor.

I pulled my chair close to Tommy's stretcher and rested my head on my crossed arms, on the sheets at his side. I must have closed my eyes for a moment.

"Mr. Thompson," he said in a soft voice. "My name is Dr. McIntyre. What is your problem today?"

Tommy told him about the pain. That immediately signaled the cardiac blood work, x-rays, and an EKG to be administered, before anything else would be done.

The pain continued.

We waited.

The curtains remained closed on the cubicle that held the second gunshot victim. None of the emergency room personnel were scurrying around in that cubicle to administer medical attention, as they had for Chief Harris.

"The other guy has got to be dead," I whispered to Tommy. "I still don't know who it is. I've got to find out."

I finally worked up the nerve to go take a peek behind the curtains.

No one was around to tell me I couldn't look, so I pulled the curtain aside and walked to the gurney. The man was dark-haired, and looked like the police officer who had pretended to be me. It was hard to tell for sure, because the gunshot damaged a good deal of his face. I looked to the side of the bed and saw the uniform. It was the police officer.

The killer was not here. He was roaming free to kill again.

I backed away from the bed and slowly closed the curtain.

My knees were about to give way again. I had to get to the chair beside Tommy's stretcher before the floor came visiting my face.

I sat and stared at Tommy. He had his eyes closed and did not see what I had done.

Should I tell Tommy that we would probably be murdered when we got to the house? No, I didn't think so. Maybe the killer took off out of town since he'd killed one cop and possibly a second one, if Chief Harris didn't make it out of surgery.

I was sure the doctor would admit Tommy to the hospital overnight for observation. That would give me time to go home and check out the house. *No, I couldn't go home tonight, my house was a crime scene.* I was sure the killer wouldn't be waiting for me at that location.

I decided to stay in one of the waiting rooms at the hospital for the night. That would be the safest place for me.

Tomorrow, I would ask a police officer to get my car for me. I was sure they had to check it for whatever evidence they could find. I hoped the car wasn't all shot up and full of bullet holes.

35

As soon as they allowed me to do so, I would go home. As soon as the doctor allowed him to leave the hospital, I would take Tommy home. Only when we were both living in the house again would we know if this nightmare was over.

That killer wouldn't be stupid enough to hang around and wait for us to return, would he?

Dear God, I wished I could see the future.

The night was long, and I was so worried about Tommy's heart. The waiting room was not the place to sleep. It seemed that all the inhabitants of our tiny town had chosen the same evening to visit the emergency room.

If I'd had my car with me, I would have escaped to the quiet of the parking lot and away from the symphony of noise cascading through the hospital.

"Oh, my God," I whispered. "Is my house still standing?"

I was again sitting in the chair in Tommy's room, listening to him breathe. Of course, he had been admitted to the hospital for observation. They were afraid not to admit him, because of his heart history. If he became too frightened, I knew there was another trip to Roanoke in my future.

I needed my car for that trip. How would I get back and forth, without my trusty Chevy Cavalier?

I forced myself up from the waiting room sofa, and went in search of the ladies room so I could throw some cold water on my face and get my day started.

I went to Tommy's room and saw that he was sound asleep. I sat as quietly as I could in the chair next to his bed.

A nurse peeked into the room and saw Tommy sleeping. She then closed the door so he wouldn't awaken.

I sat and watched him breathe, thanking God that I still had him on this earth with me.

The noisy activity in the hospital was starting to increase, so I knew Tommy would open his eyes soon.

The police released my slightly damaged car, and we went home to a slightly damaged house.

Fortunately, the bad guys didn't return to finish the job; at least, not yet.

Onward and upward to living life again.

CHAPTER 8
I HATE BEING LATE

I brought myself back out of my dangerous memories and tried to find a good memory to focus on, one that didn't involve the possible shedding of blood.

That's hard to do when the bad or scary memories seem to outweigh and outlive the good ones.

Next on the memory agenda was an embarrassing and funny moment with my best friend, Patty.

***

"I hate being late, oh God, how I hate being late," I mumbled. Frustration tinged with anger colored my voice.

If it weren't for that stupid phone call that rang into my office as I was grabbing my handbag, I would have already been at lunch with my best friend Patty, I thought. I tried to force myself not to continue talking to myself, at least not with regularity. That little aspect of my life occurred right after my husband died. I no longer had my companion, who would exchange words with me regularly. I was lucky if I exchanged greetings with two or three people on any given day, even though I was forced to work for a living. I also struggled as a designer and crocheter of angels and other items. It's a solitary hobby, thrusting my afghans into areas where I could receive possible recognition for my work.

I worked in an office where fifty to sixty people could arrive and leave daily, but I didn't see them. Most of those people had dealings with personnel, on the first floor, and never wandered up to the second floor for any reason.

My office was located at the end of the hallway on the second floor. There was no reason to be there, unless you were coming to my office. The isolation and lack of conversation with another human being caused me to voice my statements, good or bad, out loud.

The quizzical looks I would get from anyone who entered my world of one-sided conversations forced me to try to curtail my outbursts of words. This was not the day to easily control my irritation and mouth, however.

"Molly, you have a phone call," said Janie, as I walked down the steps on my way to lunch.

"Send it to my voice mail. I'm finally going to lunch," I shouted in a loud voice. "I'll have to apologize to Janie," I mumbled, letting the door slam behind me.

I was driving too fast, but I was already a half-hour late. I hoped and prayed that Patty was still waiting for me.

I rushed into the restaurant and came to a dead stop, looking for Patty. The place was full of diners, hurriedly chewing so they could get back to waiting jobs.

There was no table with a lone diner impatiently waiting for me to appear. I'd started turning to leave when I spotted her. Patty was sitting at a corner table, talking to two men. All three appeared engrossed in their conversation. Patty glanced up momentarily to give me a sign not to speak, by placing her index finger up to her mouth and slightly shaking her head in a negative fashion.

I spotted an empty table off to her right, and made my way through the crowd of eaters to get to it before it was taken by someone else. I kept my eyes down, away from her for a moment, so no one would think I was planning to dine with Patty, especially those two men sitting at her table.

Try as I might to hear, only snippets of conversation would waft towards me.

"...better not...dangerous," uttered the man with the bulbous nose and scraggily beard.

"...yeah...too bad...kill..." added his immaculate companion, dressed in an expensive suit and flashy jewelry.

I ordered a hamburger and drink so I wouldn't be so conspicuous, not to mention the fact that I was starved.

Every time the waitress fluttered around my table, she blocked the path of words. I tried not to be rude, but I wanted her out of my way.

"...now, you've got to..." said the scraggily man.

"You'd better do as...." added the slickly dressed man.

I glanced at Patty and saw how drained of color and frightened she looked. She wasn't touching the food set out before her. She was sitting stiffly in her chair, ramrod straight, struggling with her facial expressions, and so very pale.

I absently munched on my sandwich and kept a wary eye on the three occupants of the table of tension.

"Molly, Molly, over here," shouted a person who must have entered the restaurant unobserved by me. I did not recognize the voice.

I turned my head toward the sound, pulling my gaze from Patty.

"What?" I said in an unfriendly manner as I searched for the speaker of my name.

I saw no one looking at me. I knew many of the people in the restaurant, so any one of them could have shouted my name. I wasn't paying enough attention to the voice to be able to identify the culprit.

When I turned my glance back to Patty, she was gone. All three of the occupants of that table had disappeared.

I stood up abruptly, causing my chair to fall over backward and bang loudly against the floor tiles.

Startled looks were cast at me from most of the other diners.

I hurriedly picked up the chair, placing it gently in its position under the table. I kept my eyes up and searched the room for Patty.

I threw the money at the cashier, not collecting my change as I ran out of the door to continue my search for Patty. I stood in front of the restaurant, scanning the area from side to side.

"Where did she go?" I mumbled.

There was no sign of her anywhere. *Should I call the police? And tell them what? That my friend, Patty, was talking to a couple of strangers, I turned my attention to something else, and I lost track of her?*

I jumped into my car and drove back to work about fifteen minutes late.

"I'll get yelled at for that. Everyone else can be late, but I can't. The world comes to an end when I break the rules," I grumbled.

As soon as I returned to my desk, I picked up my telephone and dialed Patty's work number.

"Patty Connor, please," I told the young lady who answered the phone.

"One moment, please," she replied, as she transferred my call to Patty's line. Patty's office had not opted to switch to automatic dialing of extensions. They preferred the personal contact and opted to keep a real, live telephone receptionist employed.

I was about to hang up when I heard a click.

"Hello?" said a breathless Patty.

"Patty?"

"Hi, Molly, I'm sorry about not having lunch with you. We'll try again tomorrow," she said hurriedly.

"Who were those men, Patty?" I asked hurriedly.

"Oops, gotta go, Molly. The boss is looking at me," whispered Patty. The line went dead.

"Jeez," I whispered. I placed the telephone receiver down carefully, forcing myself not to throw it across the room and smash it to bits.

"That's it! I'm not worrying about Patty anymore," I mumbled, without any sincerity whatsoever. My mind wandered back to Patty and her two strangers all afternoon.

I tried to call her at work again, but I was told she had left early because she wasn't feeling well.

"Now I'm going to have to wait until I get home to call her. Maybe I should just pop in on her on my way," I said softly, staring at the clock. The minutes passed ever so slowly with each glance at the clock.

At five o'clock I raced out of my office and ran to my car. I would have called Patty with my cellphone, but I had forgotten to charge it last night, so I'd left it at home on the charger when I rushed to work early that morning.

I tried not to speed, but my foot was fighting the urge to step hard on the gas pedal. I slowed my speed a bit when I turned onto the street leading to Patty's house. I was looking for her car to be parked in her driveway.

It was not there. Obviously, Patty was not home.

I pulled my car over to the curb so I could watch. What I was looking for I didn't exactly know, except that I was looking for life, any kind of movement that would give me a hint as to what was happening with Patty.

I found my headphones, attached to my cassette player, and listened to a book on tape that I'd scoured the yard sales to find. Technology had advanced to CDs and MP3 players, but I still liked the tapes. I will change to the newer format when forced, but until then, I liked my books on tape. I ran the gamut with my books, from self-help and learning foreign languages to murder and mayhem, whatever I could get my hands on to keep myself entertained.

The mystery story I was listening to was just the thing to keep me alert and watching for Patty.

I knew her car was gone and that indicated that she wasn't home, but my gut told me different.

So I watched.

A curtain moved. I know I saw movement. I stared at the window, waiting for another motion sighting.

Nothing. There was no movement. *Could it have been a breeze from the air conditioner?*

I watched.

Two hours had passed, and my bladder was letting me know it was in need of emptying.

Should I leave? What a stupid question, I thought. *Yes. I have to leave, or I'm going to have to clean up a mess.*

I started my car, put it in gear, and headed for the nearest Walmart.

I was gone for fifteen minutes, at the most. When I returned, all the lights were on in Patty's house, and her car was parked in the driveway.

I pulled over to the side of the street and parked.

The lights were on, but I saw no moving shadows through the closed blinds.

Again, I waited and watched.

I couldn't stand it anymore. I had to go knock on the door. I had to see if Patty was in there. I had to know what was happening.

I swiveled my head from side to side, checking out my surroundings. I glanced at the rearview mirror to see if anyone was approaching my car from behind.

I reached toward the door handle, allowing my hand to hover before yanking it to open the door.

Was I doing the right thing? What was the right thing? I asked myself, allowing the hesitation to last for only a moment after those thoughts crossed my mind.

I climbed from my seat, again glancing around my immediate location, before I quietly closed the car door. I didn't want it to slam and announce my whereabouts to anyone in the house.

I stepped away from my car and walked toward Patty's front door.

Before stepping onto the porch I made a sharp right turn, so I could try to peek into the windows at the side of the house.

"Jeez, Patty," I mumbled when I discovered the blinds closed on the three windows on the right side.

I ducked my head, trying to convince myself that no one could see me as I proceeded to approach the small back porch. I knew that door had a window covering the upper half, so I should be able to see inside. The curtains hanging on the door were sheer and didn't block anyone from peering inside to the kitchen, where Patty spent most of her time at home, baking and cooking to her heart's delight.

Before I climbed the steps to the back porch, I could see that a large bath towel had been thrown over the curtain rod. It covered the window completely, preventing me from looking into the kitchen.

"What is going on?" I mumbled. I continued to walk around the left side of the house. Those blinds were closed, too.

I wanted to call 9-1-1. I wanted to tell them they needed to check on my friend Patty. But I knew I couldn't do that.

What would be the reason? I was worried about her. That's the reason. Wasn't that enough?

I walked onto the front porch again and pounded on her front door with my fist.

"Patty! Patty! Are you in there?" I shouted.

My fist was beginning to hurt, so I switched hands but continued to pound.

"Patty! Patty!" I screamed.

Suddenly the door opened and Patty stood in front of me, shading her eyes from the evening sun that was hitting her squarely in the face.

"What's wrong, Molly?" she asked weakly.

"There's nothing wrong with me. It's you that I'm worried about. What happened? Why are your blinds closed? Who were those two men? Why did you leave work early? Why haven't you called me? Why? Why?" I sputtered as I tried to stop the tears of relief or maybe it was anger. I wasn't sure.

"Shh," said Patty, holding her index finger to her mouth.

"Don't shush me, Patty, tell me what's wrong," I demanded loudly.

Patty moved her hands up to cover her eyes as she held the lids tightly closed.

"Migraine, Molly. I have a migraine. Please lower your voice and come in out of the glare from the sun. The brightness is making the pain worse."

I entered the dark house and saw that there was no one else there except her cat, Whiskers, who must have moved the curtain earlier. There was a blanket on the sofa.

"I was worried about you, Patty. When did you start getting migraines?" I asked in a much lower tone.

"I always had them, but they never quite got this bad. I've told you many times over the years that I've had a headache. Well, those were mild migraines. But this time it got really bad, for some reason," she said softly.

"Who were those men?" I asked.

"What men?" she asked me.

"The two you were talking with at the restaurant, when we were supposed to meet for lunch."

"The one in the suit was my brother Ted, actually my half-brother. I don't think you've ever met him. We had the same daddy. I hadn't seen him for years. That's why I never talked about him," she answered.

"They sounded like they were threatening you, from what little pieces of conversation I could hear," I said sternly.

"No, no, no threat to me. He was talking about a job he was planning to take and his buddy, Mark, was trying to talk him out of taking it, saying it was too dangerous," she explained further.

"My imagination had you kidnapped and near death. I'm so glad I was wrong. I can't afford to lose my best friend," I said.

"I'm glad you didn't call the police, but I'm also glad that you cared enough to be worried about me," Patty said with a smile.

I stood up to leave.

"Patty, you go lie down and try to get rid of that headache. I'll call you later to check on you, if that's okay?"

"Please do, Molly. I'm so glad you're my friend," said Patty. She slowly closed her front door behind me.

"Sometimes my active imagination runs away with me. Keeps life a little more interesting as each day passes," I mumbled. I walked back to my car with a smile spreading across my face, as I moved onward and glanced upward.

My memory films faded and I returned to reality.

CHAPTER 9
BINGO!

After the excitement of giving my statement about the episode in the hospital gift shop, the drive home from the police station was short and uneventful.

As soon as I unlocked my front door, I heard my phone ringing. I was brought back into the real world, my real world, with real family.

***

"Molly, I want you to go to the bingo game at the Maxwell County Fair in my place Monday night," said Maggie. She rubbed her head to try to ease the pain centered there, caused by a severe headache.

"Why, Aunt Maggie?" I asked, as I watched my Aunt Maggie suffering through one of her bad headaches. I didn't know if she had migraines like Patty, but I would be willing to guess she did.

"Does there always have to be a why?" asked Maggie.

"Yes, ma'am. You don't miss any of those bingo games unless you absolutely have to. Now—why?" I asked.

"I think Thelma is pocketing some of the money. When she goes around picking up the game money from each player for each card he or she has spread out on the table, I don't think all the money makes it back to the money counter, who determines the amount of the pot for that game," explained Maggie.

"Aunt Maggie, that's a terrible thing to say about your best friend," I said.

"I know, I know, but I don't want to say anything to her until I'm absolutely sure. I'll give her some money if she needs it. I don't want her to feel like she has to steal to get what she needs," said Maggie in a tear-filled tone.

"Okay, okay, I'll go and check on it for you. You don't think your friends will mind if I stick my nose into the group?" I asked in a skeptical tone.

"No, no, they would love to see you. They all know you, and would welcome you with open arms," said Maggie, as the tearful voice disappeared.

I watched my aunt's tears change to a smile, and knew I had been manipulated again.

"Aunt Maggie, you are so sneaky," I said. I hugged my aunt close.

"What are you talking about?" asked Maggie, with a smile that was chased away by her grimace of pain.

I loved my Aunt Maggie very much and would do anything she asked, within reason.

Checking on Thelma was a reasonable request, because Maggie and Thelma had been friends since they were little girls. I wondered why Maggie didn't just come right out and ask her.

Pride. That's the reason, for both of them. Thelma was too proud to let Maggie know she needed help. Maggie was too proud to let her best friend know that all she had to do was ask. Pride can be such a hindrance to the truth, and friendship.

I wasn't too excited about playing bingo with a bunch of my aunt's friends, not if my aunt wasn't with me.

"Oh well," I mumbled, "I guess I have to do it."

I had a hard time trying to decide what to wear to a bingo game. Should I dress down in a tee shirt and jeans, or go as a professional, in clothes I would wear to work in an office?

"Dress down, stupid," I told myself. "You're not going to a job interview,"

Jeans, tee shirt, and sneakers were my chosen manner of dress for the evening.

I wanted to check on my aunt before I moved on to the bingo game.

"Aunt Maggie, are you feeling all right?" I asked, when Maggie answered my knock at the door.

"Yes, a little better, but the sunlight is still bothering me. Come in, so I can close the door," Maggie said weakly.

"Have you seen the doctor about those headaches?" I asked, as I hugged Maggie.

"No, he isn't going to tell me anything new. Just take my pills, close the blinds, and rest," said Maggie sadly.

"I'm going to the bingo game for you when I leave here. Do you need me to do anything before I go?" I asked, with concern in my voice.

"No, no, but what are you doing tomorrow night?" asked Maggie.

"Nothing that I know of, why?" I asked.

"Would you take me to the bingo game tomorrow night? I would like to have your company if and when I have a talk with Thelma," said Maggie solemnly.

"You might not have to say anything at all. So don't worry about it. I'll pick you up at five so you can play all of the games. They don't close down until eleven, so you will have a long evening—if you feel like staying that long. Promise me you won't worry, Aunt Maggie," I said.

"I'll try, honey. I'm just worried about Thelma," said Maggie, sadly.

"I know. Well, I'm on my way and I will check on Thelma. Love you, Aunt Maggie," I said. I hugged Maggie close to me.

"Love you, too, Molly. I'm going to rest while you're at bingo. Call me when you get home," mumbled Maggie. She placed the heel of her hand against her head, searching for pain relief.

I dreaded having to go to bingo alone. I would gladly tag along with my aunt, but going alone with no one to talk to? Not my idea of fun.

The Veterans of Foreign Wars (VFW) of Maxwell sponsored a bingo fair every year, as a fundraiser for charity.

Many of the senior citizens would save their quarters to play the games, one after another, every single night of the six-day fair.

The sun was still shining as the people started gathering at the tables under the large tent.

The bingo cards were hard cardboard, designed to be used over and over again. When a number was called, the player would slide a cover over the called number on her board.

I found two cards that didn't look as worn as the others and placed them before me on the table.

Thelma was going from person to person, collecting money per card per game. According to the sign that was posted at the front of the tent, it was fifty cents for each card played.

Thelma would be collecting one dollar per game from me, because I was playing two cards.

I wasn't interested in talking to everyone. Chit chatting was hard to do, while trying to watch my cards along with keeping an eye on Thelma.

Each time Thelma picked up the money laying on the table, I saw her take it directly to the person who counted up the pot for each game. Never did Thelma pocket any of the money.

Yet the pots remained small.

They were split evenly with the VFW, but they should have been larger, due to the number of players.

"Thelma, I'm Molly, Maggie's niece," I said, trying to strike up a conversation.

"Oh, yes, Molly. I remember meeting you when Maggie was with you," Thelma said with a smile.

"How much do you collect for each game?" I asked.

"A quarter for each card. Have I made a mistake?" asked Thelma.

"No, honey, you've collected each time, but you should be taking up fifty cents per card per game," I whispered so no one else would hear me.

"When did that change?" Thelma asked, with a surprised and confused expression on her aging face.

"Last year, but that's okay. All you need to do it start collecting fifty cents each game beginning with this game," I said. I tried to encourage Thelma to continue, without disparaging her about a simple mistake.

"I'm so sorry, Molly. I didn't know I was making a mistake," she said. Obviously she was flustered by finding out what she had been doing wrong.

"Don't worry about it. It will be our secret," I said. I hugged her to reassure her.

The next time Thelma collected money from my table, she picked up the dollar for two cards without dropping any change back on the table.

I winked at Thelma and continued to play for a few more games. I felt really good about the report I was going to give to my aunt.

"Aunt Maggie, how are you feeling?" I asked as soon as my aunt answered. I made the call as soon as I arrived home.

"I'm doing better. How did it go with Thelma and bingo?" asked a worried Maggie.

"Just great, Aunt Maggie. You don't have to worry about Thelma. She isn't stealing, and she is just fine," I said, trying not to tell Maggie what the problem was.

"Well, what was happening? Why was there money missing?" probed Maggie.

"There wasn't any money missing. It just wasn't collected. She was only taking up a quarter per game per card. She's doing it correctly now. You don't have to worry anymore," I said, in explanation.

"I'm so glad. I knew you would find out what was wrong, Molly. Now we can go tomorrow evening, play bingo, and enjoy ourselves," said Maggie.

I picked up Maggie earlier than usual, so Maggie could have time to talk with her friends.

Nothing was said about the mistake Thelma had made. There was absolutely no reason in the world to embarrass Thelma in that way.

Thelma wasn't working, so she and Maggie sat side by side.

I watched the two elderly ladies do what they liked to do more than anything else in the world—play bingo.

About ten games into the evening, a loud shout was emitted by Maggie. "Bingo!"

I smiled and cast a glance upward to the stars, and my mind moved onward to happy thoughts.

CHAPTER 10
MOWING MY GRASS

The next Wednesday I got myself ready to fulfill my gift shop duty. I was hoping that I wouldn't have to hit anyone over the head this time.

I did have more visits than usual from employees, checking on me after the excitement of the prisoner's escape. I was sure they were looking for the little old gray-haired lady who hit the killer on the head.

I didn't have a chance to get bored or sleepy for those four hours. Thursday morning, I arose to a new day.

***

Spring had sprung. My grass was growing and reaching new heights.

"Dan, are you mowing my grass again this year?" I asked. Dan was the preacher who lived two doors away from my house, on the left side.

"I'm planning to, but my tractor is in the shop," he answered.

"When will it be fixed?" I asked, contemplating the height of my tall grass.

"Soon, I hope," was his reply.

"My neighbor on the right, whose name is Matt, said he would do it. I'll pay him until your mower is running," I explained.

"That's fine with me," replied Dan.

That was good, I thought. *Maybe I can get my grass cut.*

"Matt, can you cut my grass, and I'll pay you for it?" I asked my neighbor on the right side.

"Sure, no problem. Isn't the preacher doing it anymore?" he asked.

"His mower is in the shop," I replied. "He'll do it the next time."

"Okay," Matt said. I was going to get my grass cut for the first time that spring.

All was well until grass shearing time arrived again.

I didn't say anything to anybody about it, because I thought the preacher would take over the mowing again.

I had one of my all-day errands to do and while I was gone, my grass was mowed.

The mowing job was excellent. It was better than the previous mowing jobs done by Dan or Matt, but either one of them could have done it.

"Hey, Matt," I said when I saw him come through his front threshold. "Who do I owe money to for cutting my grass?"

"Your neighbor," was his response.

"Did the preacher do it?" I asked.

"No, your other neighbor next door to me," he answered.

"Who?" I asked.

"Harry," he said. He pointed to the house on the other side of his house.

"Okay," I answered.

I didn't know Harry. We had barely waved to each other, and he had been living in that house for over a year.

I walked toward the road a bit so I could see the area behind his house, where he parked his pickup truck.

"Not there," I mumbled, and returned to my living room

I messed around inside my house, glancing out occasionally to see if his truck was being driven down the street. I finished my straightening tasks and walked out front toward the street, checking to see if he had returned without my seeing him.

The pickup truck was parked there. I must have missed it when it passed my house, if it passed my house.

I walked to his front door and knocked.

"Hi, I'm Molly, your neighbor. You mowed my grass, didn't you?" I asked.

"Yes, was there a problem?" he answered in a soft spoken voice.

"No, no problem," I explained. "I need to know how much I owe you." I sputtered.

"Nothing," he said with a smile.

"Are you sure? I'll be glad to give you some money for the wonderful job you did," I said with relief. I was afraid he would charge me more than the $25.00 I was paying Dan.

"No, no money. Do you want me to do it again?" he asked. "I've lived here for over a year, and this is the first time I've talked to you."

"Sure, you can mow it. What is your last name?" I asked shyly. "Your first name is Harry. What about your last name?"

"Nelson, Harry Nelson," he said as he shook my hand.

"Thanks, Harry," I said as I turned to leave.

I smiled as I made my way back home. There was a flutter in my heart. That feeling hadn't made itself known for a very long lime.

My grass started growing again, and no one was mowing.

"Matt, what has happened? I thought Harry was going to cut my grass," I asked my neighbor when I was outside one day.

"He said he wasn't going to do it anymore. He found out you were paying the preacher, and he knows the preacher needs the money," he explained.

"But he isn't mowing my grass. You know that," I sputtered.

"Yeah, but that's what he said," added Matt.

Now, this was getting ridiculous. I knew Matt had to be the one to tell him about the preacher. Maybe it was Dan, but I don't think so.

The next day I spotted Dan.

"Dan, are you still going to mow my grass?" I asked one afternoon when I caught him outside.

"Yes, if you want me to, but my mower is in the shop again," Dan said.

"When will it be out?" I asked.

"I thought someone else was mowing it," he said.

"He was. I think he volunteered to do it because my yard looked so bad, and he wanted to meet me," I answered as I felt my skin heat up to a rosy red. "But he stopped doing it because you were supposed to do it."

"Okay, okay, I will mow your grass when my tractor is out of the shop," Dan said.

I waited and the grass grew and grew. It was getting so high that I thought one of the town council members would lodge or receive a complaint.

Matt volunteered to mow and I paid him.

As to who will do it the next time, I don't have a clue. Maybe I'll just buy a new lawn mower. I haven't had one since my son decided I shouldn't be mowing my grass. He even volunteered to mow for me, but I said no. He works a lot of overtime and he doesn't need to be worried about mom's grass.

Dan, Matt, or Harry? Who will it be? Or, should I buy a lawn mower and do it myself?

I hate to mow grass. This is my ode to the green stuff growing in my yard.

MOWING THE GRASS

The green shoots stand tall and proud
Spreading the broad blades to light.
If growing was sound—so loud
The volume would cause great fright.

The night time brings with it dew
To sprinkle and bring to life.
Strength it would always renew
Edges of blades like a knife.

Once each week, it's like clockwork.
I walk behind the machine.
It's not fun, merely just work.
It's not my plan to be mean.

The loud machine turns the blades
To chop down the growing green.
My desire to conquer fades.
I want to end this bad scene.

I still hate to mow my grass. Hopefully, my angels will help me move onward and upward past the mowing debacle.

CHAPTER 11
TRASH DETAIL

In one of my help the community endeavors, I decided to volunteer for cleanup duty at the town recreational area. I liked to volunteer and offer my help when it was appreciated, but there were times when I wondered why I did it.

***

"There are a few things you need to know before we start." I shouted loudly so they could all hear me.

I knew I had their attention with that statement. After all, what's so difficult about picking up trash?

You put the gloves on so that whatever you're picking up doesn't directly come into contact with your skin.

You don't pick up sharp or dangerous objects without approval from your supervisor. Blah, blah, blah.

They had heard it all before, because they were repeat offenders. They had each been given trash detail as punishment for not abiding by the rules.

They were all older teenagers or adults.

"First, and foremost, be careful what you pick up with your hands. You know that the world is not full of nice, clean people. Someone has to pick up after those who really don't care."

There was a muffled sound of people shifting their feet and readjusting their equipment.

"If you find anything that's questionable, don't touch it. But that doesn't mean you can't pick up a scrap of paper when you see one."

I looked at the group of uninterested people standing before me. A few were going to follow my instructions to the letter. The largest group of half-interested people in the middle were going to follow only the instructions that were useful to them. The end group, with the fewest people, would ignore my instructions in total. The end group, the disinterested people, were the ones that had to be watched closely.

This was the Monday group. This was the day of the week when there was more trash than usual to be picked up from the grounds of the neighborhood park.

Of course, our neighborhood park was a little different from what you would see in the city. Our neighborhood park was spread over several acres of land. It consisted of wooded areas, a man-made lake, and picnic shelters.

This group of fifty almost volunteers were supposed to cover the entire park and pick up every bit of detritus that didn't belong, nestled in the grasses of Mother Nature. Many of the almost volunteers were here because they had been assigned community service through the courts, social services, or the schools. Meaning that they were here as required, but they didn't particularly like their assigned tasks. They planned to only take up space, not actually work if they could get out of it in any way.

"How many of you have done this before?" I asked, already knowing the answer. "Please raise your hand if you have done this type of work, here at this park, previous to this day."

Seventy-five percent of the hands were raised into the air.

"Now, please make sure you have everything you need to take with you. You don't want to be on the other side of the park when you find out you need trash bags, do you?" I asked with a practiced smile.

The noise of equipment checking filled the area.

"You have each been assigned a number. Those with the number one, please stand over here," I said, pointing to my left. "You will be supervised by John. John, please raise your hand. John has done this before as a real volunteer. He will be able to answer any questions you might have. You will be covering the picnic grounds, and the wooded area on the left side of the park. Do any of you have any questions?"

I received several mumbled nos from group number one.

"How about the group with number two? Amy will be you supervisor. She has done this before many times as a real volunteer. Raise your hand, Amy. I want all of you to stand in the middle. You should have the most people, because you will be covering the shelters, the toilets, and the other areas where there is the most traffic."

I head the moans and groans as the middle group realized they had the most space to cover. They thought they might have the greatest amount of work assigned to them. In a way, that was true, but it was actually the assignment that was the quickest to complete, because you could see exactly what had to be done, it wasn't hidden from view, and it could be accomplished quickly. Most likely, the middle group would be the first to have their work completed, and would have to wait around while the others completed their tasks. They were all to be dismissed at the same time, regardless of when they completed their tasks.

"If they all have to work together in order to get dismissed, then those who were lagging behind would have to speed up to avoid the criticism of their fellow volunteers. Those who were going too fast would have to slow down, to wait for their fellow volunteers to catch up." I'd explained this to my boss when I volunteered to take over the supervisory duties for the clean-up volunteers.

"The remainder of you should have been given the number three. I want all of you to gather here on the right. I am your supervisor. My name is Molly Thompson. You are the lucky group today. Now, let's get to work."

From my way of thinking, people in group one were the willing workers, and would be the first to finish their assigned tasks. Group two would be a little more laid back, until Amy prodded them into action. Group three would take some mental pushing and shoving to get them motivated. Group three would be the ones who would lag behind, because they were so unwilling to complete their assigned tasks.

I started walking toward the lake, the only area that hadn't been assigned earlier. My group followed me, as they punched at each other semi-playfully and ducked and dodged from the flying fists that were issuing the punches. When they appeared to be getting too harsh with the punch delivery, I had to break up the camaraderie.

"Start looking at the ground, people. The trash isn't going to jump right into your trash bag."

They kept wanting to bunch up and work in a tight little group. That wouldn't work. They had too much territory to clean.

"Marty, you and Jenny, go to the left to about halfway around the lake. Jim and Lucy, you should go to the right about halfway, just opposite Marty and Jenny. Justin, Annie, Terry, and I will pick up around the back side of the lake, with Justin and Annie on the left, and Terry and I on the right. We should be able to get this done in no time at all. It just requires a little more walking than any of the other areas."

I was the recipient of mean, ugly looks because I broke up the little pack of people, but I needed to get this work done and splitting up the boys only and girls only packs was the way to do it. Now each and every one of them had to work with someone not of his or her choosing.

"Don't get too close to the water. This is not a day for skinny-dipping. You are all here to work."

The area around the lake, in my opinion, was the riskiest as far as accidents were concerned. I had to keep my eyes up, counting heads across the waters at all times. It made it more difficult for me to police my area, but I didn't want anything to happen to any of my volunteers. Not on my watch.

My group had scattered out. I could see them all, as they went about their business of cleaning the area of trash, cans, bottles, and whatever else we humans disposed of at a picnic.

A scream came riding the wind to my keen ears. Along with watching my brood, I was also listening for unwanted sounds that might become a problem.

I turned my head side to side, trying to determine the direction from which it had come.

Another scream, louder than the first one, was wafting through the air from the left. That direction would put it in the woods, where group one was working.

I put my hands to my mouth and shouted, "Marty, Jenny, Jim, Lucy, Justin, Annie, Terry, go to the trees! Someone needs help!"

I wasn't sure if they heard me.

I started again, "Marty, Jenny..." I was interrupted by shouts of "OK," with a waving hand from each of them. They had probably heard the scream, also.

We converged on the left side and kept moving toward the woods.

"John," I shouted, trying to locate the supervisor of group one.

"Help," was the weak response I received.

"Where are you? Keep talking so I can find you," I instructed.

I waited for John to answer, but all was quiet except for the sounds of our trekking through the underbrush.

"Group three, come over here and see if you can hear anything. You guys are younger, so maybe your hearing is a bit better than mine."

My group was ready to go and do the work required because it wasn't picking up trash. I couldn't say that I blamed them for how they felt. When the adrenaline started pumping through their veins, they were ready to rescue the world.

"Can you think of the names of any people in the first group?" I asked no one in particular.

"Yeah, Nancy and Bobby, her brother," said Marty.

"You go up ahead a little, make sure you watch your step, and start yelling their names out really loud. Pause after every yell so you can listen for an answer," I told Marty and Gerri, his work partner.

"John? Where are you?" I shouted.

No answer.

"Jim, do you and Lucy know anybody in group one?" I asked.

"Margie and Mike," said Jim. "I don't know their last names."

"That's okay, just start yelling for them over that way. I'll go up the middle, but you've got to watch your step. I don't know what has happened," I instructed.

"Yes, sure, no problem," answered Jim. He and Lucy started moving forward.

"John, where are you? We are here to help you, but we can't find you," I said loudly.

"Molly, we're over here," was the response.

The voice sounded like it was right in front of me. I couldn't see anybody standing where I thought the voice should be.

"Where?" I asked.

"In a hole, in the ground," said John weakly.

I looked down, but saw nothing that looked like a hole in the ground.

I was almost afraid to move forward.

"Group Three, watch for a hole in the ground. Make sure you watch where you put your feet," I admonished. "Break off a sturdy stick and punch on the ground in front of you."

"Over here," said Marty. He was off to my left, not out of sight. I could still see him.

"What is it?" I asked, as I started moving toward him.

"There's nothing under this disturbed brush. It looks like solid ground, but there's nothing there."

"John, are you all in there?" I shouted.

"Yes, and Missy is hurt. She fell in first. We all sort of tumbled in after her. Please be careful, so you don't fall in with us," John said breathlessly.

"Marty, you stay here with me. Jim, you go back and get some rope out of the storage building. Lucy, you go to the office and tell them to call the rescue squad, the police, the fire department, and anybody else they think can help. The rest of you, stay with me. We'll see if we can get any of them out," I said as I ushered them off to their individual errands.

"Come on, all of you left here with me, we need to find out where the hole in the ground begins and ends, so we can clear away the brush and get our volunteers out of trouble. Continue to use your sticks to poke at the ground. Let me know when you have no ground, so we can mark the area. Pull up as much of the brush as you can, and give it a toss away from the area," I told them, as my eyes searched the underbrush.

Slowly we poked at the ground, all the way around where we figured the hole to be.

"You guys down there, move back from where the edge is hanging over you, so we can start pulling the brush away," I yelled as I started yanking at the greenery growing in front of me. There were enough of us to clear the area away. It was soon almost clean, with only long rooted growth remaining, minus the leaves and small branches.

We were looking at an almost perfectly round hole in the ground.

"What does it look like down there?" I shouted.

"A tunnel," shouted John. "It might have been an old mine shaft, or maybe a tunnel leading to the stills that used to be built in this area many years ago. I can't really tell, it's too dark."

"How far down are you?" I asked loudly.

59

"Maybe ten feet. It couldn't have been too far because we all lived through the fall, if you know what I mean," John explained.

"Marty's here with a rope. Do you think any of you can climb out?" I asked.

"No, too scared," said John.

"Okay, just hang on. The rescue squad will be here soon, and I know they can get you all out of there. How is Missy doing?" I asked.

"She's crying. Her ankle is really swollen up. She might have broken it," said John.

"I hear sirens. You're getting the help you need, right now," I said with all of the encouragement I could muster.

"Thank God!" shouted John.

We all backed away from the hole, allowing the people trained to rescue the fallen from the hole.

We watched intently.

None of us were leaving until we saw the very last volunteer pulled from the hole.

When the ambulance pulled away to go to the emergency room with Missy, I turned to my expanded group of wonderful volunteers.

"You all can go home now. You have done a wonderful job, even if you didn't get it finished. Don't worry about it. I can take care of it tomorrow. If you have a job, make sure you go to work tomorrow so you can move on and file this away in your mind as mission accomplished," I said, a grateful smile spreading across my face.

The crowd broke up, and all were on their different paths toward home. They would all have a good story to tell.

I, too, needed to go home and let the adrenaline rush fade away. I knew I would have a hard time trying to sleep, but eventually the excitement would dissipate.

Early the next morning, I was determined to complete the work that had been left undone, all by myself.

When I arrived at the park, almost all of the group I had sent home with incomplete tasks were waiting for me. They had readied themselves for the day of work.

I couldn't have been more proud of my almost volunteers.

My volunteer angels led me onward and upward through the day.

Chapter 12
I KNOW WHAT I SAW

My next angel afghan show was for my hometown of Maxwell. It was the day of the Main Street Moments Heritage Festival, and I was sort of obligated to show up. It was a good obligation. It made me feel wanted, and that was wonderful.

We usually didn't have many displays of bad conduct, but this time ugliness reared its bold head and a simple act turned into a disaster.

***

"I saw him hit her, and I mean hit her. I could hear her teeth clash together. Then I saw her fall down," I told Officer Charlie Martin. He worked for the Maxwell Police Department, and was standing in front of me to ask questions about the incident.

"What happened next?" asked the officer.

"He drew back his foot and kicked her in the ribs," I said.

"What next?" the officer urged.

"I started screaming my head off. I wanted someone to stop him. I knew I wasn't able to do it, but a man could have. A policeman with a gun could have shot him. That would have stopped him, all right," I said, a little louder than normal.

"Did you recognize the man?" asked the officer.

"No, I never saw him before. I hope I don't ever see him again. He is vicious, and dangerous," I added.

"Do you know what brought on the attack?" asked Officer Martin.

"No, she wasn't doing anything. He just ran up to her and starting hitting," I explained.

"Did he say anything to her?" Officer Martin asked.

"All he said was 'this is payback,'" I answered.

"Payback for what?" probed the police officer.

"I don't know. Angie never told me that she was having any kind of man trouble," I answered.

"What makes you think it was man trouble? What kind of man trouble?" he asked.

"It was a man beating on her. Wouldn't you think it was man trouble?" I asked.

The policeman shrugged his shoulders, but gave no verbal answer.

"Would you be able to recognize him if you saw him again?" Officer Martin asked.

"Sure, I looked right at him. But it happened so fast. What if I'm wrong?" I answered.

"You might have to come to the station to look at some pictures, or help us draw a sketch," Officer Martin suggested.

"No problem," I said.

"Can you describe him for me?" asked the officer.

"I thought you wanted me to look at pictures," I said.

"I do, but any additional information will help. What did he look like?" Officer Martin asked.

"He was white, of average height, with what I call dirty blonde hair that was graying around the edges," I said.

"How was he dressed?" the officer asked.

"Black, faded jeans and a black, long-sleeved tee shirt. He had on white sneakers," I said.

"What about his head? Did he have anything on his head?" asked Officer Martin.

"No, nothing. That's why I could see his dirty blonde hair," I answered.

"Is there anything else you can remember about him?" asked Officer Martin.

"No, not at the moment," I answered.

"Let me have your complete name," said Officer Martin.

"It's Molly, Molly Thompson," I said.

"You wait right here, ma'am. I'm going to go talk to one of the other witnesses. I don't want you to leave until I say you can go. I may have some more questions for you," he said as he walked away.

I nodded my head in acknowledgement. I knew my two lady friends were going to tell the policeman the exact same thing I told him. They were standing next to me. They saw the same thing I did.

"I'm Officer Charlie Martin. What is your name?"

"Gerri Hampton," she answered.

"You saw me talking with your friend Molly. Now, I want you to tell me what you saw," said Officer Martin.

"What did Molly tell you?" asked Gerri.

"She told me what she saw. Now I want to know exactly what you saw," said the officer.

Gerri looked flustered. She didn't want to be involved in all of this commotion. She didn't know Angie very well. What were all of Gerri's church friends going to think?

"Well," she said hesitantly, "I saw him running towards Angie. I don't know if it was intentional, but he crashed into her and her head went back. The force of the hit caused her teeth to rattle, and she went down like a rock."

"Then what?" urged Officer Martin.

"The blow to Angie, caused by him running into her, made him miss his stride. When Angie fell to the ground, he couldn't get out of her way and he bumped into her with his foot. He almost fell over her," explained Gerri.

"You're saying he ran into her. It was an accident?" asked Officer Martin.

"Yes, that's what it looked like to me. Isn't that what Molly said?" asked Gerri.

"Did you know that running man?" asked the officer.

"He looked a little familiar. I don't know why, though. Maybe I'm confusing him with someone else. It happened so fast," said Gerri.

"Would you be able to pick him out of a photo display?" asked Officer Martin.

"No, I don't think so," Gerri said hesitantly. "I didn't get a good enough look at his face."

"Can you tell me what he was wearing?" asked the officer.

"Well, let me think. I need to get a picture of him in my mind," explained Gerri as she closed her eyes to ponder the answer to his question.

"Ma'am, anything will be of great help," said Officer Martin, trying to hurry her thinking process.

"Just one more second, sir," mumbled Gerri. "There...there it is. I have a clear picture of his back and side. He didn't seem very tall," she said as she continued to hold her eyes tightly closed. "He was wearing blue jeans; a blue and white striped short-sleeved pullover, and dark colored tennis shoes. Does that sound about right?"

"It's not a question of sounding right, ma'am. I need to know what you saw. That's all," he answered as he frowned at the words he had written down on his small notepad. "Did you see his hair? What color was his hair?"

"He had no hair. His head appeared to be shaved, or he was completely bald. I don't think he was old enough to be completely bald, but you never know these days," said Gerri.

"Did he say anything?" asked Officer Martin.

"Nothing I could understand," Gerri answered.

"Is there anything else you might want to tell me about this man?" asked the officer.

"Yes. I think he was Hispanic," said Gerri.

"Really?" asked Officer Martin.

"Isn't that what Molly told you?" Gerri asked.

"No ma'am, it isn't," answered Officer Martin.

"I know what I saw," added Gerri.

"I'm sure you do," said Officer Martin as he turned to glance into the direction of witness number three. "Don't leave just yet. It won't take much longer. I need to talk to your other friend. You can join your friend Molly, if you would like."

Officer Martin approached the third witness with dread. He had been told many times that eyewitnesses were very unreliable, but this was the first time he had really seen such a disparity between the descriptions.

"I'm Officer Charlie Martin. I need to get some information from you about what happened when your friend was hurt. Let me have your name, please."

"Peggy Rollins," she answered.

"Okay, Ms. Rollins, describe what you saw," said Officer Martin.

"You've talked to Molly and Gerri. I'm sure they gave you an accurate description of the event. Why would I need to give you another one corroborating the same story?" questioned Peggy, in her own peculiar way.

"Both ladies have told me their interpretation of the event, but I need yours just to make sure that all three of you are on the same page. Now please, Ms. Rollins, begin with the moment you saw the assailant," urged Officer Martin.

"You called him an assailant. I don't know if that was what he was. There was someone chasing him, and he ran into Angie full force. I don't think he could stop himself," explained Peggy.

"You mean it wasn't intentional?" asked the officer.

"No, Angie was in his path," she answered,

"Did he strike her?" asked the officer.

"He appeared to make a motion with his right arm. I think he was trying to get her to move at the last moment before the collision," said Peggy.

"So you're saying the whole scene was merely an accident," said Officer Martin.

"Yes, but there was someone chasing him. Once he ran into Angie, that someone left my field of vision and I didn't see him again," explained Peggy.

"Can you describe the man who was chasing the one who ran into Angie?" asked the officer.

"No, no way. I just caught a glimpse of him," explained Peggy.

"How about the one involved in the collision?" asked Officer Martin.

"What do you want to know specifically?" asked Peggy.

"What was he wearing?" continued the officer.

"He was running until he smacked into Angie. When he knocked her down, I didn't pay any attention to him. I was concerned about Angie," said Peggy.

"You don't remember anything about how he was dressed?" probed Officer Martin.

"Well, yes, but I'm not real sure. I wouldn't testify to it in court," said Peggy.

"We need any help we can get, ma'am," urged the frustrated police officer.

"I remember khaki shorts and a pale yellow muscle shirt. You know, the kind of shirt that has no sleeves. It looks like an old-fashioned underwear shirt for a man. He was kind of short. That's all I can remember. He was just a blur, and I wasn't paying attention to his clothes, Officer," said Peggy,

"Yes ma'am. What about his hair?" asked Officer Martin.

"It was black, long and bushy looking, like he hadn't combed it for days," said Peggy.

"Anything else? Can you remember anything else at all?" asked the officer.

"He was wearing brown sandals," Peggy added.

"What about his skin color?" asked Officer Martin.

"White, of course," Peggy said.

"Is that it?" asked Officer Martin. He rubbed at his head while holding his hat cocked over to the side.

"Officer Martin, what did Molly and Gerri say?" asked Peggy.

"Ma'am, I don't believe any two out of the three of you were looking at the same event. The descriptions aren't even close," replied Officer Martin. He immediately regretted answering that question. He should have said nothing. He knew that, but he was so aggravated with what he was hearing from what appeared to be three intelligent, respectable women that it slipped out.

"What do you mean?" demanded Peggy.

"I'm sorry, ma'am, I can't talk about the details," he sputtered.

"That's fine with me. I'll just ask my friends to tell me what they said," snapped Peggy, with a definite sarcastic tone.

"I'd rather you didn't do that, compare notes I mean. The investigation is still ongoing," he explained.

"It's not against the law, is it?" asked Peggy.

"No," Officer Martin answered.

"Then I guess you can't stop us from talking to each other. After all, we are friends, and the three of us work together every day. We will be talking no matter what you say," Peggy said emphatically.

"Yes ma'am," said Officer Martin with a nod of acknowledgement. He wasn't about to argue with the lady. She seemed a little too defensive to suit him.

Peggy turned away from Officer Martin and walked directly towards her two friends and coworkers.

Officer Martin saw them gesticulating while they talked. He knew there was trouble brewing by the way their hands were flying around and the volume of their voices, which had increased with every retort. He watched the ladies for a while, until the group broke up and headed in three different directions. Then he decided he needed to go to the hospital to check on Angie, before reporting to the Chief of Police.

Officer Martin stood in front of the automatic double doors to the emergency department barely out range of the electric eye that would initiate the opening action of the entrance. He watched for a few moments so he could determine where all of the action was happening. He was sure they would still be making life saving efforts on the prone form of Angie Simons.

He spotted the busy cubicle in the trauma area. The curtains were drawn completely around it to shut out prying eyes.

Officer Martin stepped forward to activate the doors.

No one paid any attention to him. They were busy scurrying in and out of the curtained cubicle.

"Mary?" he said in a loud whisper.

She didn't hear him.

"Mary, I need to ask you a question," he said, standing in front of a woman dressed in brightly-colored scrubs.

"What do you need, Charlie?" she said cheerfully.

"Is Angie Simons in there?" asked Officer Martin. He pointed towards the curtained area.

"Yes, I think that's her name," said Mary.

"Is she able to talk to me?" Officer Martin asked.

"Not now, she's unconscious. What actually happened to this woman?" asked Mary, with a display of interest.

"That's what I'm trying to find out," he said.

"You had better talk to the witnesses," said the nurse. She turned away from the officer.

"I did, but they were no help, believe me," he said in a disgusted tone. "When should I come back?"

"Couple of hours," said Mary. She disappeared behind the curtains.

"Mary," shouted the officer, "call me at the office if she wakes up before I get back here."

"Will do, Charlie," Mary replied, from behind the curtain.

Officer Martin sat in his police cruiser and looked at his notes.

"How could the stories from the witnesses be so different?" he mumbled. Then he drove the short distance to the police station.

"Hey, Chief?" Officer Martin said.

"Yeah?" responded a masculine voice.

"You got any idea how three ladies can look at the same scene and tell me such totally different stories?" said a confused Officer Martin.

"Now, remember when I told you that eyewitnesses can't be trusted?" asked the chief.

"Sure I do, Chief, but I didn't think the stories would be so wide apart, if you know what I mean," said Officer Martin.

"Did you talk to the victim?" asked the chief.

"No, she's unconscious. The hospital will call me if she wakes up before I get back," explained Martin.

"That's who you need to talk to, you know," said Chief Harris.

"I know, Chief. I know. I just hope she does wake up. She's pretty bad off," said Martin.

Officer Martin pulled his notepad from his pocket and stared at the words he had scribbled onto the paper. He was determined to make sense of what the three women witnessed.

"Chief, this is what I have. Can you help me try to put it together?" Martin asked.

"I'll do what I can," replied the Chief.

"To start with, they don't agree on the race. Two of them say he's white, but one says he's Hispanic. At least they agree on average height or shorter," said Martin.

"I'd go with a short, tanned, white person," said the Chief with a smile.

"They do not agree at all on the hair, or if he even had hair. One says he's dirty blonde. I'd call that a light brown, but you know how women are. Another says he has long, bushy, dark hair. The third says he has no hair," continued Martin.

"Short, light brown hair sounds like a good compromise to me," added the Chief.

"Next it's the clothes, and that's really strange, too. Black jeans and a long-sleeved black tee from Molly, blue jeans with a white and blue striped shirt from Gerri, and khaki shorts with a yellow muscle shirt from Peggy. How do you make sense out of that?" asked Officer Martin.

"Dark blue jeans with a yellow or black tee shirt," responded Chief Harris.

"White sneakers, dark tennis shoes, or sandals; which one would you guess?" asked Martin.

"Beige sneakers, because of one of them said she saw sandals," said the chief.

"Okay, now I'll go to the scene. One said it was an intentional assault. Two say it was an accident, with one of those two saying he ran into Angie purely by accident because he couldn't stop himself in time. The other said someone was chasing the man who basically ran over the victim. Again, it was unintentional," said Officer Martin.

"Charlie, my gut tells me it was no accident. I would have to say it was purposeful," said Chief Harris.

"Well, that leaves us with a tanned, white male who was holding a grudge against Angie Simons. He had short, brown hair and was wearing dark blue jeans with a yellow or black tee shirt, and beige sneakers," said Officer Martin.

"Are you sure it was a man? You all just assumed that, didn't you?" asked the Chief.

"You don't think a woman did this, do you, Chief?" asked Officer Martin.

"Why not? A woman running fast enough and hard enough could do just as much damage as a man could," suggested Chief Harris.

"I never thought about it that way, but I guess you're right, Chief."

"Like I said earlier, Martin, you need to speak to the victim."

"That's what I'm going to try to do right now," said Officer Martin. He walked through the door, headed towards the police vehicle.

When Officer Martin entered the emergency room, the high-speed activity he'd seen earlier had dissipated. A couple of the cubicles were occupied, but obviously they weren't the type of emergency the medical personnel had faced with the arrival of Angie Simons.

"Mary, where is Angie Simons?" asked Officer Martin.

"Intensive care," Mary said.

"How is she doing?" asked Martha.

"Not good. She has a brain injury," replied Mary.

"Did she gain consciousness?" asked the officer.

"For a few moments, but then she was out again. Doctor says she's in a coma," said Mary.

"Does he expect her to ever wake up?" asked Officer Martin.

"He doesn't know," said Mary. She shook her head for emphasis.

"I'm going over to ICU to poke my head in, and let them know I need to talk to her when she wakes up. See you later, Mary. Thanks for the information," Officer Martin said as he turned to leave.

Wires and hoses were attached all over Angie Simons. There wasn't any part of her frail body that they weren't monitoring.

"I'm Officer Martin," he told the nurse sitting behind the desk. "I need to question Ms. Simons as soon as she is able to talk to me."

"That won't happen for a while. She's in a coma, but she is showing signs of trying to wake up," said the nurse.

"How long do you think it will be?" asked Officer Martin. "You'll need to talk to her doctor, but it will take her a little bit longer to get fully awake, if she does wake up," said the nurse.

"What are her chances of waking up?" asked Martin.

"I'd say it's fifty-fifty, but you never know with brain injuries. Even if she does wake up she may not be able to tell you anything because of memory loss, which is pretty common," replied the nurse.

"Has she said anything?" probed Officer Martin.

"Yes, she keeps saying a name over and over again," said the nurse.

"What name?" he asked.

"Lisa," replied the nurse.

"Do you know who Lisa is?" asked Martin.

"No," said the nurse.

"Call me at the police station when she wakes up. I really need to talk to her. Ask for Officer Martin."

"Yes sir," said the nurse.

He contemplated his next step as he drove the short distance to the police station. He pulled his notepad from his shirt pocket as soon as he reached his desk, and started making phone calls.

"Peggy Rollins?" asked Officer Martin.

"Yes, this is she," Peggy responded politely.

70

"Officer Martin here. Your friend Angie Simons keeps whispering the name of Lisa. Do you know who Lisa might be?"

"No, I'm sorry. I don't know any Lisas," said Peggy.

"Thank you," said Officer Martin. He disconnected the call and immediately entered Gerri Hampton's number.

"Angie keeps saying Lisa. Do you know who Lisa is?" Martin asked.

"Let me think," said Gerri.

Officer Martin could see her in his mind, closing her eyes and willing herself into deep thought.

"No, no, I don't think I've heard her talk about a Lisa. I don't know any Lisas, as a matter of fact. How is she?" Gerri started to ask about Angie's condition, but her conversation was abruptly ended.

"Thanks," he said. He disconnected Gerri and entered Molly's phone number.

"Molly Thompson? This is Officer Martin. Do you know anyone named Lisa?"

"Lisa who?" I asked.

"That's what I'm trying to find out," said Officer Martin.

"Angie has a sister named Lisa Simons. I don't think she's married yet, so it would still be Simons. Has anyone contacted her?" I asked.

"No, ma'am, we didn't know she had a sister. Do you have her number?" asked the officer.

"I believe she's staying with Angie," I said.

"What is Angie's number and address? I have the information off her driver's license, but her phone number wasn't on it, of course. I just want to double check the address, if you have it," said Officer Martin.

"Sure, no problem. I'll get them for you," I said. I pulled my address book from my handbag.

Officer Martin decided not to call the number I had given him. Instead, he drove to the address and parked on the opposite side of the street. He wanted to watch the house and get a feel for the area.

He saw the curtain move—maybe. He was far enough away from it for movement to be hard to distinguish.

Then he saw it. Someone was running away from him, down the street.

Officer Martin went into cop mode and took off after the running figure in his police car.

The running person glanced back at his car, but never slowed.

He started the siren and lights, hoping the frightened runner would slow or stop.

The runner turned right, down a narrow alley. Fortunately for Officer Martin, it was a dead end. The runner had nowhere to go, and turned to face the oncoming vehicle head on.

Officer Martin jumped out of the vehicle and approached the frightened runner, with his gun drawn as a safety measure.

"Are you Lisa Simons?" Officer Martin asked.

The runner was leaning over gasping for breath.

"I asked you, are you Lisa Simons?" he repeated.

"Yes," she answered breathlessly, eyeing the gun cautiously.

He watched her closely. He was not sure if she was pretending to struggle for breath to prepare herself for a rapid take off or not. He holstered his gun and watched her every movement.

He made a mental note of what she was wearing; navy blue blouse, blue jeans, and dirty once-white sneakers. Her brown hair was pulled back in a ponytail, with loose wisps falling across her face.

He finally understood why the descriptions were so different.

"Why are you chasing me?" Lisa asked. She still struggled with trying to gain control of her breathing.

"I need to talk to you about your sister," said Officer Martin.

"Is my sister okay?" Lisa asked.

"No ma'am. She's in intensive care, and the prognosis is not too good for her coming out of the coma," explained Officer Martin.

"Coma? Angie's in a coma? Why?" asked a worried Lisa.

"When you ran her down, she hit her head and was pretty bruised up," explained Officer Martin.

"I didn't mean to hurt her. It was just a game we've played since we were kids," sputtered Lisa.

"It's a little rough, isn't it?" asked Martin.

"I guess I really caught her off guard. Normally she sidesteps me and comes running after me. When I knocked her down, I kept running because I knew she would catch up with me and return the favor. I had no idea she was so badly hurt. Then, when she didn't come home, I didn't know what to do," said Lisa.

"Why did you run from me?" asked Officer Martin.

"I was scared," Lisa replied.

"Why?" asked Martin.

"When I came back to town, I had left a bad relationship at college. I took a couple of things that used to belong to my boyfriend, but he gave them to me. When I left, he wanted them back, but they were mine and I was keeping them. It wasn't much, just a ring and a necklace. I thought he sent the police after me to collect his possessions," she explained.

"Did you intend to cause your sister harm?" asked Officer Martin.

"God, no, never. It was just a game," said Lisa. She wiped at the tears that were filling her eyes.

"I'll drive you to the hospital to see Angie. Get into the back of my vehicle," said Officer Martin.

Officer Martin walked with Lisa through the hospital to the ICU waiting room, where he left her sitting while he checked in with the nurse.

The nurse led Officer Martin and Lisa Simons into the ICU, where they could see Annie's prone form. A multitude of hoses, wires, and monitors of all kinds attached to her frail body made her look even smaller on the elevated hospital bed.

Lisa was crying softly, uttering Angie's name and rubbing the exposed area of her left arm.

Angie's eyes fluttered and you could hear a distorted "Lisa" whispered, despite the tubes in her nose and mouth.

Officer Martin left the room and mentally closed the case.

"It was just a game," he mumbled.

When I found out the outcome of the game, I was shocked that something so simple could go so far.

I believe the angels were present to help both sisters, or they both could have succumbed to death.

Life in my small town kept rolling onward and upward.

CHAPTER 13
CHIEF, I'VE GOT A PROBLEM

I drove home from my day at the Virginia Highlands Festival, where I managed to sell an angel afghan, a couple of scarves, a baby layette, and two rag rugs. It was a good day, and I actually had a little bit of money in my pocket.

I was smiling when I turned the car into my driveway, but once my eyes focused on my kitchen door, a frown appeared on my face.

It was open! The back door to my house was standing wide open. I lived alone, so absolutely no one should have had any reason to be inside my house.

I was afraid to get out of my car and enter my kitchen. I didn't know who or what would be lying in wait for me.

Just out of my sight, around the corner of the house, I saw a glint of bright sunlight bouncing off of a super shiny object. I inched my car forward to try to catch a glimpse of the shiny object.

Suddenly I froze. Panic filled me.

"I've got to get out of here," I mumbled. I slammed my gearshift into reverse.

My car jerked with my sudden stomping on the gas pedal. I recklessly backed out of my driveway, without looking in either direction for oncoming traffic.

I drove down the road toward the heart of my little town of Maxwell, in search of the police chief. I was not observing any of the speed limits. I just needed to get to the police station as soon as possible.

I parked in the lot behind the police station. I wanted to hide my car from view from the street. I glanced around me before I climbed out of my vehicle, just to make sure no one had followed me.

"Is Chief Harris here?" I asked, walking through the back entrance.

A young lady dressed in a dark brown police uniform responded. "He's in his office." She waved me on, motioning toward his office.

"Molly, come on in," said Chief Harris when he saw me.

"Chief, I've got a problem," I whispered excitedly.

"What's that, Molly?" he asked.

"They're back," I answered.

"Who's back?" he asked.

"The motorcycle people," I said slowly.

"What are you talking about, Molly?" he asked as he looked puzzled.

"Remember that trouble Tommy and I had a few years ago, with the motorcycle gang that was trying to kill us?" I asked.

"Yeah, what about it?" he asked.

"I saw a motorcycle parked behind my house a few minutes ago. I'm afraid to go home. I'm afraid that freak has come back to finish the job," I said with a sigh.

"I'll go check your place. You stay here until I get back," said Chief Harris.

"Take someone with you, Chief," I cautioned.

"I will. Just stay here," he ordered.

"Be careful," I said, as he left me sitting in his office.

I worried about what would happen if Chief Harris confronted the motorcycle gang members. For that matter, I wondered how many members of the gang were actually at my house.

It took Chief Harris an hour to return, with no one in custody.

"What happened?" I asked, when he entered the office where I had been waiting for that long, long hour.

"Nothing. There was no one there. I saw no sign of anyone being there, and your back door was closed and locked. Are you sure you saw a motorcycle there?" he asked.

"Of course I'm sure," I said. I could feel my anger rising.

"I think you can go on home, Molly. You should have no trouble at all," he said in encouragement.

"Sure, okay, Chief Harris. I'm sorry I bothered you. Have a great day," I said sarcastically as I left his office. I didn't mean to be sarcastic, but I know that was what it sounded like.

No way was my day going to end on an onward and upward note.

Chapter 14
THE MOVING VOICE

I wasn't going to go home. I wasn't ready to face the fright again. A trip to the mall was what I needed, to allow me to fortify myself and work up the courage to face my fears.

I entered the store with only the thought of wasting some time, fortifying my backbone a bit before heading home.

The lights went out and the darkness slammed into me so quickly that my breathing stopped for a few moments before I gasped for a fresh intake of air.

"Hey! What happened?" I shouted.

"Don't know," said a masculine voice to the left of me.

"I can't see a thing. I'm afraid to move. I don't want to break anything," I said.

"I know what you mean," added the same masculine voice, except this time it came from directly behind me.

I blinked my eyes, hoping that the simple motion would clear the darkness enough so that I could see the owner of the moving voice.

I slid my foot forward a couple of inches as I held my hands out in front of me, reaching for anything that would be in my path.

"Where are you going?" asked the voice.

I could almost feel his breath caressing the back of my neck.

I didn't answer.

I was standing inside a gift shop that had no source of light other than the light fixtures overhead, which were not working. This particular gift shop was filled with delicate glass items, displayed on glass shelving, and any movement in the wrong direction on my part could cost me a bundle of money.

I extended my hands and forced myself to turn completely around, trying to get my bearings. I was safe so far. I wasn't going to knock anything over where I was standing.

I moved a few inches to my right and did another cautious three-sixty. I felt my hip brush against a shelf, but nothing crashed to the floor. Now I knew which way I had to move, to try to get to the front of the store. At least, I thought I knew where the front entrance was located.

I moved ever so slowly in the opposite direction from where I felt the presence of the shelf. I was afraid to slide my foot. I didn't want the person with the moving voice to be able to hear the brushing of my shoe against the carpet, and know in which direction I was traveling. For that matter, I could be traveling towards him without even knowing it.

I stepped forward again, hoping and praying I was not moving into the trouble I was trying so desperately to avoid.

"You're going in the wrong direction," said the voice.

"How would you know?" I demanded.

"You're going to knock over a shelf if you keep it up," he cautioned.

"Again, how would you know? It's dark in here. You certainly can't see any better than I can," I said.

"No, I can't see in the dark, but I've been in this store many times. I'm quite familiar with it," he replied.

"Okay, Mister Know-it-all, how do I get out of here without totally destroying the place?" I said, not even pretending to hide my irritation.

"Just stay where you are. I will come to you, and lead you to the front door," he said calmly.

I didn't know whether I wanted to do that or not. I knew I had never met this man before, because I didn't recognize his voice.

I couldn't stand there locked in this position all day. I needed to move. At the very least, I would need to go to the ladies room soon.

"Okay, but no funny stuff," I said firmly.

I stood waiting for him to grab my arm and lead me to the door that would take me into the common area of the mall, where I was sure I could find my way to an outside door that would allow me to make my way to my car.

He touched my arm gently and whispered, "This way to the daylight."

My spine tingled and my knees weakened a bit with his touch.

"Thanks," was all I could get myself to say.

I hadn't had a reaction like that, the tingly spine and weak knees, since long before my husband died. Then I thought about how much time had passed since his death. It had been about six years. It was about time my heart started to heal and look for a new beginning.

As soon as we crossed the threshold from the dark, isolated world of the gift shop into the wide common area of the mall, the lights popped on and I could see the man making me feel tingly with his touch.

He was a gentleman who looked to be in his early to mid-sixties, slightly balding, with a ring of white hair. His face was ruggedly handsome and his blue eyes sparkled with happiness.

"My name is Molly," I said quickly, turning slightly to make eye contact.

"I'm Mack," he said

"Thanks, Mack, for guiding me out of the store. Are you the custodian here at the mall?" I asked as I glanced at his khaki-colored work uniform.

"Yes, Molly, that's why I know this store as well as I do," he answered.

"How long have you worked here?" I asked.

"A long time; several years, but I'm not usually here in the middle of the day. I'm glad I had to come in today, to repair a shelf in the back room. I actually got to help a lady in real distress," he said, with a smile that seemed to light up his face.

"Thank you again, Mack," I said. I made myself move away from his gentle touch on my arm.

"Molly, are you married? I noticed you weren't wearing a ring," he asked shyly, in a tone just barely above a whisper.

"No, I'm a widow. Have been for about six years," I replied eagerly.

"Would you allow me to take you to dinner one evening really soon?" he asked.

My heart was fluttering. I was a teenager again; a sixty-six year old teenager.

"That would be wonderful," I answered. I hoped I wasn't appearing too eager.

We both walked through the mall exchanging phone numbers and addresses, and talking about everything and nothing for about an hour longer, until I realized I was late for an appointment.

I drove home that evening with a smile on my face, instead of the frown of loneliness I had endured for six long years.

The telephone startled me from my daydreaming about enjoying life again.

"Hello, Mack," I answered softly, after I glanced at the caller ID.

"Hey, Molly. What are you doing?" he asked cheerfully.

"Thinking about how lucky I was to be stranded in the dark in that gift shop," I said with a giggle.

"Me, too," he replied.

My mind whirled with excitement, stopping on a phrase I had avoided for such a long time. I smiled.

Life was good again. It was moving onward and upward.

CHAPTER 15
SHOW YOUR FACE

Reality smacked me in the face when I remembered exactly what I had chosen to forget. Mack was a good momentary diversion but fear, once again, reared its ugly head.

I had been so school-girl excited about meeting Mack that I'd neglected to check out my house. My gut was telling me I needed to be worried. I shook my head to clear my brain.

"Stop it," I told myself. I rose from my comfortable seat on the sofa. "Chief Harris said everything is all clear, no motorcycle gang members. Just go to bed," I mumbled loudly.

I closed all of my window blinds and checked both doors to see that they were locked. I walked down the hallway to my bedroom and my cool, comforting sheets.

It didn't take me long to complete my nightly duties and crawl into my bed. In no time at all, I was sleeping soundly.

Suddenly I was awake. I was wide-eyed, looking around, trying to figure out what had actually brought me out of my sound sleep.

I heard nothing.

I saw nothing in the darkness.

I knew something or someone was there, because I could feel the presence of some kind of life form.

"Who's there?" I whispered.

No answer.

"I know someone is here. Show your face," I demanded. I tried to sound brave; not scared, which was exactly what I was.

No answer.

I scrambled from my bed in the dark and reached for my robe, lying on the chair next to the end table with my house slippers tucked underneath it.

I knew someone was in my house. I thought about dialing 9-1-1, but what would I say? I felt a presence, and that was all. I had seen no one and I had heard no one. How could I tell the police that someone was there when I had no proof yet?

I was sure they would think I was a crackpot. I had already sent them on a wild goose chase once.

I walked toward the bedroom door in the dark and stuck my head out into the hall. It was darker than usual because, for some unknown reason, my night light was not shining its seven watts of lovely light.

I ducked back into my bedroom to think. I didn't know what to do.

The closet—I should go hide in the closet. Getting under the bed was out of the question for these tired, old bones. I found the closet door and turned the knob slowly.

"Please don't squeak," I prayed as I pushed some of my clothes aside to force my wide body in behind them

Then, I waited.

I tried to silence my breathing. I wanted to hear him coming. I wanted to hear his sneaking footfalls on the carpet in the hallway.

I heard nothing; no sounds at all.

After hiding for about thirty minutes, I was becoming a little claustrophobic. I had to get out of that hole in the closet.

I inched the clothes hanging in front of me over carefully, so there was hardly any sliding sound. I stepped forward, fighting my way through the clothes and quietly opened the closet door. After pushing the door open slowly and cautiously, I peeked from the confines of the closet into my very dark bedroom.

I saw nothing in the darkness, but I could still feel his presence.

I froze when that feeling hit me again. I didn't know what to do next.

I hate being indecisive.

I knew I had to get out of the closet, no matter what or who was waiting for me.

I stepped out, expecting my world to come to an end.

My hanging clothes grabbed at me, clinging to me, like they were trying to stop my forward progression. I brushed at the clingy, filmy blouse that was hanging onto to me and turned my head to listen for sounds from the hallway.

I knew there was someone there. God help me, I knew there was a stranger in my house.

In my mind I could see him stop to listen each time I stopped to listen. That's why I couldn't locate him

I moved forward into the hallway, praying that my old, creaky floors didn't squeak like they usually did. First one step, stop and listen, then another step, stop and listen, until I reached the doorway to the living room.

I poked my head through the doorway, and felt a breeze filtering its way through the room from the front door, which was slightly ajar.

I froze for a few seconds, staring at the open door.

"Move, stupid, turn on the light, now," I mumbled, reaching for the light switch.

The brightness blinded me for a moment. I shook it off and quickly scanned the room.

There was no one there. He could be hiding in another part of the house, but I didn't think so.

I felt some of the tension drain from my body as I ran to the front door to close it and lock it up tight.

I moved over to the window nearest the door facing the street, where I saw two police cars parked with lights flashing. They appeared to have pulled over a car for some unknown reason, and I was ever so grateful. The flashing lights were probably what forced my night visitor out of my house.

I looked through my house one more time, so I would feel safe enough to go to bed.

I tossed and turned in my bed as I tried to figure out how my night visitor got into my living space.

I knew I'd locked everything before I went to bed the first time, so how did he get inside?

CHAPTER 16
SEARCHING FOR ANSWERS

At six AM I gave up trying to sleep. I crawled out from beneath my scrambled bedcovers and proceeded to the kitchen to make some eye-opening coffee. I needed it to get primed and ready for my day of searching for answers.

While the coffee brewed, I took a quick shower. This was my normal routine before embarking on my daily duties, which were what I chose to do because I was retired.

Showered and refreshed a bit, I walked through my house once again. I had to find out how he had entered my living space, and what I had to do to eliminate his re-entry.

My house wasn't very big space-wise, but I had three bedrooms, a kitchen and dining room combination, and a living room. My house had fifteen windows, a front door, and a back door.

I started in my bedroom. I planned to work my way around the house, stopping at the back bedroom, located next to mine.

I checked both windows in my bedroom. There were no signs of disturbance around them, so I went on to the living room, where there were four windows and the front door. Everything looked fine and nothing was out of place, so I went on to the small dining area I had converted into an office for my desktop computer. The two windows were locked up tight, with no disorder surrounding them. The kitchen window was high up over the sink, so I didn't expect to find anything there.

The back door was right off the kitchen. I gave it a thorough going over, but nothing was scratched or broken so that wasn't the entry point.

I was about to give up, but I still had two more rooms to check.

There was no kind of entry through the bathroom, so I walked into the second bedroom. It only had one window. Nothing—there was no sign of entry or disturbance.

It had to be the third bedroom, which was beside my room. The two were separated by closets, so I probably wouldn't have been able to hear anyone climb in through one of the two windows. The first window I checked was undisturbed.

The second window was another matter. I could tell it had been forced open. The table in front of the window had been moved out of place; not much, but enough for me to notice. When I raised the window, I didn't have to unlock it. The lock had always been broken, but I had wedged a piece of wood in the side of the window to make it immovable. That piece of wood was gone.

I walked outside to check the window from that vantage point, but it was too high off the ground for me to see any marks made by forcing the window open.

He must either have been really tall, and strong enough to pull himself inside the house through the high off the ground window, or he carried a ladder with him. If he rode his motorcycle, he could have parked it under my window and used it as a step up high enough to get inside.

From the appearance of the marks in the grass and on the ground, that was exactly what he had done.

I hadn't heard the sound of a motorcycle, so he must have pushed it around my house to where he needed the boost.

Back in the house, I found my hammer and a couple of large nails. No one was ever going to get into my house through that window again.

CHAPTER 17
THAT SOMEDAY IS HERE

I sat on my favorite chair in my living room, drinking my coffee after eating my breakfast of cold cereal.

I thought about how my night visitor had been to my house twice already, but none of my neighbors saw him either time. If they had caught a glimpse of him, they would have been pounding on my door to check on me. That was the kind of neighbors I had, and I was very happy they kept a watchful eye out for danger.

My mind went back to the time my husband and I were almost arrested for prowling around a stranger's house, and the fact that we did get caught.

***

"Someday your curiosity is going to get you into trouble," whispered my husband. He stood behind me, allowing me to lead him into that same trouble.

"You want to know, don't you?" I said.

"Yeah, but we can find out when he's ready to tell us," he added.

"When will that be?" I asked.

"I don't know, soon I would think," he said.

"I can't see anything. How about you? What can you see? You're taller than I am," I whispered.

I scrunched down as far as I could so he could see over the top of my head.

"It's dark in there. I can't see anything, except my own reflection in the window glass," he said. He cupped his hands around each side of his face to shut out the glare from the street light that was behind us.

"No movement? Not even a night light? Eddy told me he left a night light on all the time for the cats. It must have burned out," I explained.

"Let's move to another window. It's really hard to see anything through this one," Tommy said. He backed away from the window, allowing me to straighten up and move out of the strain I had been forced into with him peering into the window over me.

We walked around to the other side of the house, where we found a window that was lower to the ground. I planted my face smack up against the window, cupping the sides of my eyes to block any glare.

I jerked back suddenly, nearly knocking Tommy to the ground.

"There's something or someone in there," I whispered.

"What? Let me see," Tommy said. "I don't see anything. What was it?"

"I don't know. Whatever it was it moved past the window fast, really fast. I couldn't tell if it was man or beast," I answered.

"Did it have a shape?" he asked.

"No, it was fast, more like a blur," I said softly.

"Did it look like Eddy?" Tommy asked.

"No, well maybe, I really couldn't tell," I answered. "Maybe there's someone in the house who shouldn't be there. Maybe someone is trying to rob Eddy. I think we should call the police."

"What do we tell them?" Tommy asked.

"What do you mean?" I said.

"Do we tell them that we were peeping into Eddy's house because we wanted to see his new home? We haven't been here before. Nobody knows us around here. Do you really think the police are going to believe us?" asked Tommy.

I guessed Tommy was right. What would we say to a cop who might be asking questions about two grown, over-the-hill, adults posing as peeping Toms?

"Let me see if I see anything, since you can't tell me what it is you saw," said Tommy.

87

"No, not here. Let's go to the back of the house. We'll probably be able to see more. That was the direction whatever it is I saw was moving towards. I really need to know what or who that was. If it is Eddy, why doesn't he just let us in?" I asked.

"What's wrong with you?" Tommy asked, as he watched me forcing my chubby body into an almost stealthy form.

"Someone's watching us. I can feel it. Eyes are watching our every move," I whispered.

"Molly, who would be watching us?"

"I don't have any idea, but I can sure feel those eyes boring holes into me," I said.

"Maybe we should turn around and leave. Right now, let's leave," whispered Tommy as he glanced around looking for those eyes.

"No, we're here at the back of the house now. We need to take a look before we scram out of here," I said.

The windows seemed to be higher off the ground. I didn't think that was really true. The fact was that the ground sloped down toward the back of the lot.

"Look around, Tommy, see if you can find something to climb on. I won't be able to see a thing. The top of your head will just barely reach the window ledge."

"I see a metal lawn chair. I'll grab it. We'll take one little peek, and then high tail it out of here. Okay?" said Tommy.

Tommy dragged the chair to the area beneath the window.

"That's okay right there, Tommy. Let me climb up and look inside."

"No, I'm going first this time. You can just wait a minute," he said as he stepped up onto the seat of the metal chair. "This thing is wobbly. Stand over here beside me so I can steady myself."

"Okay, but hurry up. I want to see, too," I said.

"I can't see anything, Molly. Are you sure this is Eddy's house?" he asked.

"Yes, I wrote the address down," I answered as I dug into my pocket. "See, it's 6150 Baptist Valley Lane."

"Okay, okay, but there's something wrong here," he said. He stepped off the chair so I could climb up to peer into blackness.

I saw nothing but a back area of the house that quite possibly used to be a back porch. It was now enclosed to become a mudroom and storage area.

"Well, let's try the door. It might be unlocked," I said.

"Molly, no, we can't do that," whispered Tommy harshly.

"Why not? Eddy is our son," I said.

"Then what are you going to do? Snoop around inside? Why don't you clean his house for him?" Tommy said sarcastically.

The door knob turned and I glanced at Tommy. That was when I noticed a tall, uniformed figure standing behind my husband. He was pointing the biggest hand gun I had ever seen directly at Tommy's back. He was holding it in a stance that told me he would shoot if we provoked him in any way.

"Tommy, we have company," I said softly.

Tommy's face blanched to a bloodless white. He raised both hands and backed away from the door.

"Officer, can my husband sit down? He has a bad heart condition," I said. I pushed him down onto the step we had climbed to get to the door knob.

"Yeah, okay, what do you two think you are doing?" asked the officer.

"Our son lives here. We wanted to take a peek and see how he has his rooms decorated so we could get him some housewarming gifts. He just moved here about two weeks ago. We've haven't been invited to visit yet. But we wanted to have the gifts in hand, when we finally get that invitation," I explained with a rapid burst of words.

"What is your son's name?" asked the officer.

"Eddy Thompson," I replied.

"The person who lives here is not Eddy Thompson," said the officer.

"Oh," I said. I could feel my blood rise through my veins and rush to my face, turning my skin a bright shade of red.

I dug into my pocket and pulled out the address I had scrawled onto the piece of paper.

"I had his address written down," I said as I handed it to the officer.

"You two wait out front. Stand next to my vehicle. I'll check with the owner of the house and see if he wants to press charges," the officer said. He walked to the front porch and banged on the door.

Tommy's color returned, to the opposite extreme. He was now red-faced and very, very angry.

"Molly, I told you this was a bad idea. I told you your curiosity was going to someday get us into trouble. Well, that someday is here."

"I know, I know. But it's too late to worry about that now," I said in a calming tone.

The officer walked slowly from the house toward the two of us, standing next to his police car.

"The owner of this house thinks you've reversed the last two numbers of the address. He thinks you need 6105, not 6150, Baptist Valley Lane. He also said he saw a rental truck, used for moving household goods, parked in the driveway at that address a couple of weeks ago."

"Maybe I did. I tend to do that at work. I bet I reversed those numbers when he told me his address over the phone. I'm so sorry. Are you going to arrest us?" I asked.

"No, it was a mistake. I'm sure of that. But don't go snooping around your son's house without an invitation. His neighbors might call us for a return trip. Anyway, the guy who lives here did the right thing, calling the authorities. Some of the rednecks who live in this county would have shot first and then asked questions. So don't be doing this again," he said sternly. He tipped his hat and walked away, with a hint of a smile trying to turn up the corners of his mouth.

"Let's go home, Tommy," I said, leading my beloved husband to the car. "I promise to rein in my curiosity."

Beneath my breath I finished the sentence, "Until the next time."

***

I knew people made mistakes, because we did.

This was not a mistake.

The man who entered my house was planning to do me harm. There was no doubt about that.

I hoped my angels were hanging around. I needed help to move onward and upward.

CHAPTER 18
A KNOCK AT THE DOOR

I roused myself from my memories and made a decision to go see the chief of police again, even if he thought I was a crackpot or a frequent flyer. That's how they refer to one of those people who cry wolf too often. I had to have help from someone. I'd started to get ready for my visit to the police station when I heard a knock at the door.

I panicked. I was expecting a visit from no one I knew.

I was frozen in place, unable to move. Only my brain was functioning, and it was sputtering like a defective fuse about ready to smolder and die.

If I stood there not making a move, maybe the person knocking would go away and leave me to my task. I knew I was quiet. No one should have or could have heard me moving around on the carpeted floor.

"Mrs. Thompson, are you in there?" asked a deep, masculine voice.

I slapped my hands over my mouth to keep myself from answering.

"Mrs. Thompson, open the door, please," said the voice with a little more firmness.

I knew it wasn't the police, because the knocking man would have told me that detail.

I was rooted to the carpet, in the space between the door and the front window of the living room. I knew he couldn't see me, unless he had the ability to peer through walls. I didn't think he had acquired Superman attributes. Perhaps he had Superman **hearing and could** hear me breathe.

I tried to quiet my breathing, for fear that he might hear my excited intakes of air along with the rapid exhale.

I did not move. The floor boards might squeak.

A frightening thought raced through my mind.

What if he had a key?

Where would he get a key, stupid? My mind was now answering my questions.

"Mrs. Thompson, you're going to have to talk to me eventually. I hope you know that. I'll go away this time, but I'll be back," said the voice, losing strength. It wasn't as loud as it had been. Maybe he was walking away from my front door.

The back door...Maybe he went around to the back door.

I dropped to the floor, on my hands and knees. I made my way to the kitchen door to make sure I'd relocked it when I checked the house.

The windows in the kitchen opened the room up to the outside world. It also opened up the view for anyone wanting to look inside from the great outdoors, and see anyone or anything walking around in the room. I forgot about how open it was. There were windows on three sides, with no place to hide from anyone who decided to scan the room.

I remained on all fours as I crawled into the kitchen. I knew I could be seen even if I stayed on all fours, but I had to check that door.

I turned my head at the slightest noise, but unfortunately it wasn't the noise of the cops that I was hearing. House creaks and settling noises along with the refrigerator hum and the seconds clicking off of the electric clock were the sounds of the kitchen.

"Thank you for not checking the back of the house," I whispered, as I stood up to rest my sore knees. I was not used to racing around on all fours. My skin was a little tender on the knees. "I'm getting too old for this," I said. I thought about how ridiculous I must have looked. This sixty-plus overweight body trying to move around on all fours like an infant learning to crawl must have been quite a sight to see.

The tears started flowing and I couldn't stop them.

How did I get into this mess? How was I going to get out of it?

I got back down on all fours and crawled from the kitchen to the living room, where I could sneak a peek out of the front window. I needed to see that the knocker was gone. I gently pulled the curtain aside to get a good view of the expanse of street, from my neighbor's house on the right side to my neighbor's house on the left side. I saw no one.

I stood up again, much to the relief of my aching knees.

"I'm not going to tell the police about anything, what I saw or didn't see last evening. I think it's better that way. Let them figure it out when I'm dead," I mumbled. I raced back and forth from room to room, looking out the windows.

I finally wore myself out to the point that I could lie down and take a nap. I needed one. It was quiet. I refused to turn on the television or the radio, because both small appliances made noise and that might prove to the outside world that I was home.

I was jarred awake by someone pounding on my front door. My heart was racing and the pounding knock nearly scared me to death. I looked around me, trying to figure out what I was doing in this room. It was not my bedroom. I was in the guest bedroom. Why was I in this bedroom? Then the knocking started up again. I knew why I was hiding in this room.

"Mrs. Thompson," the knocker bellowed. It was the same voice, from earlier in the day. "I know you are home. Your car is parked out back. You wouldn't go anywhere without your car. Let me in so I can ask you a few questions."

"No," I whispered, knowing that he couldn't hear me nor could he see me. "Go away!" my mind shouted, but the words never left my mouth.

"Mrs. Thompson, I'm going to be sitting in the front of your house. I'm not leaving until you come out to talk. All I need to do is talk with you. That's all, Mrs. Thompson. Then I will go away and leave you alone."

The longer he was making noise at my front door, the angrier I was.

The room that I was hiding in was a small room, and the walls seemed to be closing in on me. I knew I couldn't stay in this room very much longer. That was what fear could do to me. It made me really paranoid and afraid of silly, stupid things.

My cellphone rang and startled me out of my fear of moving walls. I grabbed for the phone quickly so the knocker wouldn't hear the soft ringing sound.

"Hello," I whispered.

"Molly? Molly? Is that you?" asked a concerned voice at the other end of the connection.

"Yeah, who is this?" I demanded in a loud whisper.

"Patty. It's me, Patty."

"Oh good, I need to talk to you," I said, a little louder than I should have.

"Is everything okay, Molly?" asked Patty.

"There's a strange man beating on my door. He won't go away until I talk to him, Patty," I said in a flurry of rapid words.

"Do you want me to call the police?" Patty asked.

"Yes—no—wait a minute. The knocking and shouting has stopped. Keep hanging on until I check outside my door," I whispered.

I looked out the window closest to the front door, and saw no one standing there.

I raced to the back door, glancing out windows as I passed them. I saw no one.

"I think he's gone," I whispered into the telephone.

"Who?" asked Patty.

"I don't know. I think it was the same guy who broke into my house last night," I said.

"What are you talking about? Who broke into your house?" Patty asked.

"I truly do not know, but I think it's the same motorcycle gang member who tried to kill my husband and me a few years ago," I explained hesitantly.

"Did you call the police?" Patty asked.

"No, not last night," I answered softly.

"Why not?" Patty demanded.

"They couldn't find anyone or anything the last time I called them. Actually I went to the police station in person, I didn't call them. I was so embarrassed, but so afraid. I didn't want to embarrass myself again," I explained.

"To heck with embarrassing yourself, Molly. You could have been raped or even killed," Patty said loudly.

"I know, I know, but he's gone now," I said. I fought hard to hold back the tears.

"If you don't call the police, I will. Do you understand what I'm telling you?" Patty asked firmly.

"Please don't call the police. He's gone now. I promise to call them if he returns," I whispered.

"I'll be calling you again to check on you," Patty said.

"Okay, please do. I want someone to miss me if something happens," I said. I cast my eyes upward, looking for help to force myself to move onward.

CHAPTER 19
THE EMPTY STAGE

I knew I shouldn't have said that out loud, my miserable thought about needing someone to miss me, but I really couldn't help it. I was beginning to feel sorry for myself, with plenty of reason, and the words just had to come out of my mouth before I burst.

"Patty, let's change the subject. I've got a couple of free tickets to go see the music festival at the baseball stadium in Bluefield. Do you want to go with me?" I asked. I crossed my fingers, hoping she would say yes.

"When is it?" Patty asked.

"Later this afternoon. There are supposed to be several bands there," I said, with excitement rising in my voice. I hadn't actually planned to go, but I decided it was better than staying at home and being scared and worried. I was sure my night visitor, the motorcycle gang member, wasn't going to attack me in a crowd.

"I can't, Molly. I have to go to Roger's mom's house for dinner. If I had known in advance, I could have made different plans," she said in a scolding tone.

"Sorry, I wasn't planning to go, but all of the scary business makes me think I will be safer in a crowd," I said apologetically.

"You really are worried, aren't you?" asked Patty.

"Wouldn't you be worried?" I snapped.

"Yeah, I guess I would be, but I really can't go. I'll go with you on your next excursion," Patty said softly.

"If there is a next time," I mumbled. "See you later, Patty. I'm going to make a couple of calls to see if someone else will come with me," I said, a little louder.

"Bye, Molly," said Patty. "I am sorry."

"No problem," I said. I disconnected the telephone and placed it back in its cradle.

I knew no one else would go with me on such short notice, so I made a decision I wouldn't normally make. I decided to go alone. It wouldn't be as much fun, but I could pretty well stay hidden in the crowd.

I changed into jeans and a tee shirt, then donned comfortable sneakers.

There must have been thousands standing in the rain that day. Well, it looked like thousands. Actually it was just a few hundred, which was still a big number for our small town of Maxwell. We were all standing around, staring at an empty stage.

Some had umbrellas. They were the fortunate ones; then again, maybe not. The rising winds were wreaking havoc on the umbrellas by turning them inside out, or threatening to pull the handle holder up into the air like Mary Poppins.

I was one of those without an umbrella, a raincoat, or any kind of protective gear. I stood staring at the empty stage, dressed only in jeans, a tee shirt, and sneakers.

Needless to say, the wet tee shirt was revealing much more of my body than I approved of, so I crossed my arms in front of me. Then I grabbed my elbows, holding on to hide some of my physique.

I continued to stare at the empty stage, knowing full well that no one was going to be performing any kind of entertaining show for those people stupid enough to continue to stand in the rain. There were many of us stupid people doing just that. I guess we were expecting the skies to clear and the sun to shine enough to dry up all of the water that had fallen to the ground.

I had handed over my hard-earned money for a music show that wasn't going to happen. I had to talk myself into going alone, but I did it. I wanted to see what I had tickets for, and I wanted to see it now, rain or no rain.

A chant started behind me.

"We want Travis...we want Travis...we want Travis..." said one voice, then two voices, then many voices.

"We want Travis," I chanted with the crowd. That little bit of activity was helping me to stay warm. The cold rain was causing me to chill. I stomped around the ground where I could find a spot that wouldn't splash cold water up to my jeans, soaking me even more. I wasn't trying to reinforce my displeasure with the empty stage. I was only trying to warm my cold body with the heat of movement.

"We want Travis...we want Travis...we want Travis," continued the crowd.

A person walked onto the stage and the chanting stopped abruptly.

There was no microphone, only the man shouting.

"Ladies and gentlemen. Your attention please! Ladies and gentlemen, we are canceling the performance today. It will be rescheduled for a later date. Hang onto your ticket stubs, and you can use them again at that time. Thank you," said the shouting man. He turned on his heel and abruptly walked off of the stage.

The crowd started to buzz again. It was not a gentle buzz. It was an angry bee buzz that was getting louder and angrier.

The crescendo of noise was amazing to hear. One or two voices spread through the crowd and grew into a multitude of jeers and shouts.

The mood was rapidly changing from a group of wet, rain soaked, impatient people to an angry, stomping, shouting crowd who wanted their demands to be met. I was in the middle of that angry crowd, and I definitely was not happy.

Suddenly a mud ball flew through the air and splattered against the back wall of the mobile stage. As water and mud streaked down the wall, my heart was sinking inside my chest with the same speed.

I had no idea who threw the first mud ball, but I saw many of the people standing behind me adding to the mess with more globs of mud. If I hadn't ducked when I saw one of the mud balls racing toward me, I would have been hurt.

The crowd was moving forward, pushing closer to the empty stage.

There was absolutely no way I could stand my ground. The momentum was too strong.

I was being pushed forward by the crowd. I looked around me as I tried to figure out which way I should run, so I could get to my car and out of danger.

I sidestepped to my left, trying to break away from the forward movement. That step helped a bit, but not enough to get me clear of the surging crowd.

Again, I sidestepped, and when I looked behind me I could see the crowd was no longer extended toward the back. It had spread out side to side, building up a stronger forward momentum.

I was trapped.

I could no longer sidestep my way to my car and safety.

I had no desire to be part of any angry, destructive mob.

"Why did I have to come see this stupid old show?" I asked myself. I continued to look for an avenue of escape.

Someone hit my back. It didn't feel like a mud ball. It actually felt like a fist. Why would anyone hit me like that? I tried to turn around to see my attacker, but I was being squashed into place by people on each side of me.

"Stop it!" I shouted as I swung my arms towards the people at my sides.

My right arm smacked someone in the stomach, because I heard a whoosh of breath. My left arm brushed against a person's side. Both people glared at me—if looks could kill, I'd have died on the spot. I needed to move away from those killer stares.

"Let me out of here!" I shouted, trying to move left.

There was a small opening, and I scooted into that little hole. It moved me a couple of feet closer to safety. The further left I moved, I noticed that the bodies were not packed as tightly together, so I kept forcing my way through the milling bodies. I didn't want to anger anyone enough to strike out at me. I'd had enough of that. All I wanted to do was go home.

Suddenly I heard sirens.

Some of the bodies took off running toward their cars, into the same parking lot to which I had been headed. I thought they were all scattering and scrambling for the exits, leaving no one inside the stadium to cause more destruction.

"Oh no, the police," I mumbled. I continued to move toward my car.

I spotted my car and ran to it.

I opened the driver's side door, jumped inside, and turned on the ignition. I slammed the car into gear and drove to the exit, dodging running bodies who were not watching behind them to see a moving car aimed at them. The exit rose up in front of me like a beacon, leading me to find my way out of trouble

"Please let me get out of here," I prayed as I turned onto the street.

I looked behind me to catch a glimpse of flashing lights that would be pulling me over to the side of the road.

"So far, so good," I whispered as I drove onto the entrance ramp to Route 460.

I was shaking. It had never been my intention to become a part of a mob. I merely wanted to watch Travis Tritt sing his songs.

Sirens could be heard all over town, as police cars raced to the stadium to quell the rioting mob. I couldn't believe they were still in there. Why?

News bulletins interrupted the country music station's onslaught of golden oldies with forceful announcements. "Do not go near the baseball stadium, because it would only add to the confusion with the possibility of eminent arrest. If you need to pick someone up, do not attempt to do so at this time," shouted the announcer.

I cringed at the thought that it must have gotten more intense after I sneaked out of there.

I knew my guardian angel had helped me get out of there, and I was extremely grateful.

The mud balls could have easily escalated into something more danger-ous, even deadly. An angry mob can get carried away, leading to damage and destruction to fulfill the need to strike back at those who had ended the rain soaked, out door concert.

"This is a news bulletin from KING Country. Do not attempt to go near the baseball stadium at this time. An angry mob has succeeded in overturning the portable stage, injuring some of the concert attendees in the process. Any concert attendee who remains in the stadium at this time will be taken to the police station for questioning. Charges will be made after the cameras located throughout the stadium have been viewed. Family members will be contacted after the questioning is complete."

When I arrived home, I cried with relief and thanked my angel for her help.

"Never again," I mumbled, when I managed to get myself to calm down a bit.

Later, I tuned to the local news and a truly horrible sight.

The mob had overturned the mobile stage and a couple of police offi-cers had been injured in the melee.

I recognized some of the people I knew from my small town being hauled away in handcuffs.

"That could have been me," I mumbled, watching in disgust.

Angels were beginning to become more and more a part of my thoughts. I was glad it was angels filtering into my thoughts and dreams. I couldn't think of anything or anyone that could have helped guide me onward and upward into my life.

'

CHAPTER 20
THE GIFT

I walked onto my front porch, and was surprised and disgusted to find a dead baby bird. My guess was that Cloudy, my gray and white cat, was making it her responsibility to feed me again by leaving me a gift.

My mind wandered back to the short story I had read about three cats. Strangely enough, the cats in the short story all had the same names as my cats. Perhaps I had subconsciously picked their names based on that short story. My cats are, Cloudy, Jughead, and Wild Child. They have more or less taken over my life, not allowing me to sink into depression most of the time.

***

The story begins:

Ladies and gentlemen, we are watching Jughead, the big black and white beauty, escort his ladies, Cloudy and Wild Child, through the perils of the green grass of the front yard. Juggy thrusts his head into the air and searches his surroundings before he beckons the ladies to follow him further.

Wild Child is the timid one, but the largest in size of the three felines strutting through the greenery. Her blue-gray coat is thick and heavy, and her green eyes blink as she prepares to turn and run at the slightest sound.

Cloudy, a white and gray spotted beauty, is much trimmer than her niece, Wild Child, but is not afraid of most things unless they are bigger than she is.

Forward they travel, until Cloudy sees something that is amiss in the grass. She springs forward and grabs for the movement.

Cloudy pulls her head back; her mouth is filled with a writhing, wiggling snake. She aims her body towards the front porch, where she drops her gift for her master onto the concrete floor. She keeps a watchful eye on her treasure.

Wild Child has long since left the scene to hide in the flower bed, while Juggy watches with disdain.

When Mavis, the owner of the house, opens her front door, she does not notice Cloudy's gift.

Out of the corner of her eye, Mavis sees something move. She isn't looking at it head on, so the movement is all she sees.

"What is that?" she screeches, jumping back from the wriggling object.

Cloudy demurely lowers her head and scoops up the wriggling object.

"Cloudy, that's a snake!" shrieks Mavis.

Cloudy clinches her jaw tightly around the small snake as it whips around, trying to bite her.

"Take that thing out of here," hisses Mavis.

Cloudy steps closer to Mavis as she tries to present the gift of a living, wriggling, snapping snake to her caretaker.

It finally occurs to Mavis that she must acknowledge the fine gift from Cloudy, and praise her for her wonderful contribution to her nutritional needs.

Mavis grimaces as she reaches toward the top of Cloudy's head.

Cloudy drops her gift and raises her head to accept the rubbing that Mavis is proffering.

The snake tries to recover and retreat, but Cloudy would not allow that to happen.

After a few more bites from Cloudy, the snake succumbs to its beating and no longer struggles to escape.

Again, Mavis rubs the purring Cloudy who is joined by Juggy and Wild Child so they, too, can participate in the love fest.

As soon as the cats are no longer watching the snake, Mavis picks it up with a shovel and drops her gift into the garbage can, ever so grateful that Cloudy loves her enough to want to take care of her.

***

I thought of how throughout history, cats had gotten the wrong end of the deal when they were branded familiars to witches and warlocks.

My cats were akin to the angels who pushed me onward and upward while watching after me. Of that I was absolutely sure.

CHAPTER 21
BLUE EYES

After I disposed of Cloudy's gift, I called Patty to see if she would go to dinner with me. I was looking for human companionship, not feline.

Of course Patty was busy, but I didn't want to be home alone. Anyway, I wanted to check on my lawyer friend, Tim Walker. Besides the fact that I wanted to know legally what I could do about my night visitor, I also wanted to know what was up with him. I had left messages at his office and received no response. That was not like Tim. He was my lawyer, but more importantly, he was my friend.

It was a short drive to the establishment where he and his legal cohorts would hang out.

The sound of a motorcycle made me want to duck down and hide from sight.

Why would that gang member come after me at this late date?

***

My right eye opened, and then my left eye struggled to peel the upper lid from the lower lid. I rubbed at my left eye, trying to force it open. I closed my right eye and brought my right arm up across my forehead, with my fingers reaching toward my upper lid. Then, I raised my left hand up so my fingers would be able to tug at the lower lid.

I could feel the upper lid start to peel away from the lower lid. Finally, it opened far enough so that I would be able to see out of it.

My head was pounding with intense pain, throbbing in waves. I knew there was no reason for the pain. All I drank last night was tomato juice, doctored up to look like a Bloody Mary.

I looked around me and realized I wasn't in my own bed.

I threw back the sheet that was covering me and saw that I was in my bra and panties. No nightgown, but not completely naked, thank God.

The room was filled with furniture that wasn't new, but it also wasn't junk store stock.

The drapes were drawn and looked a bit sun-bleached. They were clean, or as clean as you would expect them to be in a motel room.

I moved quickly to crawl off the queen-sized bed, on which I had been sleeping.

Quick movement was a mistake.

I sat on the edge of the bed and waited for my brain to stop spinning. It was making me sick, the spinning movement in my head.

I stood up slowly and staggered to the bathroom, where I hung my head over the porcelain throne.

Having eliminated what little bit of fluid I had in my stomach, I splashed cold water onto my face. I walked slowly from the bathroom in search of my clothes. I found them folded neatly and stacked on the large dresser.

I found literature in the form of a couple of brochures extolling praise for the motel, Super Eight.

I thought I knew where I was, probably Claypool Hill, Virginia.

Now, I just had to find out why I was here.

I lived about twenty miles from Claypool Hill, so there was no reason for me to rent a motel room and not drive myself home, especially when I was not drinking.

I found no conspicuous fluid secretions on my thighs, so my thoughts were that I as not sexually molested.

"Thank you, God," I whispered as I glanced upward.

I checked inside drawers of the dresser, in the small closet, and in the bathroom. I even looked under the bed.

My handbag was nowhere to be found, not in this room, anyway.

I opened the door and discovered I was facing the parking lot.

I walked out into the full, bright sunlight and squinted my sore eyes as I looked at every car in the lot. There were about ten vehicles parked at odd angles, but my old tan Chevy Cavalier was not there. Something else was missing. I didn't see a motorcycle. There should have been a motorcycle parked in the lot. That's what my mind was telling me.

I walked to the office.

"Hi, I'm Molly Thompson. I'm in room 110. I really need some information," I explained. I looked the desk clerk in the eye.

"How can I help you?" The young lady asked.

"Were you working last night, Amber?" I asked, when I caught a glimpse of her nametag.

"No ma'am," Amber said.

"Could you tell me who checked me into 110?" I asked.

"Pardon me?" she asked.

"I don't remember checking in. I need to know who put me into 110," I tried to explain.

Amber looked at me with disgust as she walked to the computer and pulled up the information.

"You paid with cash and because you had a local address, we didn't need a credit card," she answered.

"Did I give you my name?" I asked.

"You had to. It's in here as Molly Thompson," she said.

"Did I come in alone?" I continued.

"I don't know, but if you were that drunk, you probably needed help," she said sarcastically.

"I wasn't drunk, because I don't drink," I snapped at her.

"Oh? Then why can't you remember anything?" she said not too politely.

"I don't know," I whispered softly. "Did anyone turn in a lost handbag, and do I owe you anything?"

She glanced at the clock and replied, "No to both questions."

"One more question," I said.

"What?" Amber said impatiently.

"Did I give you my driver's license for identification?" I asked.

She glanced at the computer and said, "No."

I had been in Maxwell when I was drinking my Virgin Mary, a nonalcoholic Bloody Mary. I remember nothing after that.

I had been sitting at Donnie's Place, talking to acquaintances about the upcoming Christmas holidays. I had an ulterior motive for being there amongst people I didn't particularly care about.

I was trying to find out what happened to my attorney friend, Tim Walker.

When I called the law firm where he held a partnership, I was told he was on an extended vacation. That reason for absence didn't quite fit the Tim I knew. He was a workaholic.

I couldn't imagine why any of those fine upstanding citizens would add something to my drink. If they did, what was it? Besides, the fact was that I thought my current predicament was due solely to the man on the motorcycle.

I left the motel office and went in search of my car. I stood on the sidewalk and looked around me, trying to find out where I could have parked my car.

I know I must have been a strange sight. I had done the best I could to straighten my disheveled appearance before I left room 110.

I walked to the corner where there was a traffic light that would allow me to cross a busy, car-filled Route 460. I noticed that the occupants of the vehicles I walked in front of were dressed in what I would call their Sunday finery. It looked as if they were going to church.

"What happened to Saturday? Did I sleep through it?" I mumbled. I made my way to the local Walmart.

I hadn't asked Amber what day it was and she didn't volunteer the information. I'm sure she thought I knew it was Sunday.

I wanted to search the Walmart parking lot in the hope that I would be able to find my car.

I quickly surveyed the many parked vehicles without spotting my tan Chevy. I would have to walk up and down each row to make a better search.

As luck would have it, I found my car parked in the last row. Since I didn't have my keys, which were hopefully in my handbag, I got down on my hands and knees and reached for the spare. It was attached under the front wheel well, on the passenger side of my faithful Cavalier.

A couple of people walked past me and cast me some questioning glances.

"Got a leaking tire," I said, as a possible explanation.

They walked on, and I continued my key hunt.

"Found it," I mumbled. I jerked it loose from its moorings.

By the time I crawled up from the ground, my hands and knees were shaking. I inserted the key, opened the door, and fell onto the driver seat. I still was feeling under the spell of whatever got me into this state.

I glanced over to the floorboard on the passenger side, and there was my handbag. I grabbed it and peered inside to find my wallet.

"It's there!" I shouted with astonishment. I jerked my wallet open to see that my credit cards and cash were still in place. "I wasn't robbed. What in God's name happened to me?" I asked the empty car.

I knew I needed to backtrack and find out what happened. I pulled my appointment book from my handbag, and flipped through the pages until I got to Sunday.

The beginning of this nightmare happened on Friday night. I checked my calendar and found nothing on Friday, Saturday, or Sunday. It was a free weekend, so I knew I would be able to stay late at Donnie's Place and do some investigating on my own.

I was not trained in criminal or missing person investigations by anyone other than what I had read in books or watched on television.

In other words, I was a friend trying to find a friend by the name of Tim Walker.

I decided my next step should be to go to the emergency room at the local community hospital.

My medical problem was that I lost part of Friday, all of Saturday, and part of Sunday. That warranted a drug screening if not more, in my opinion.

I drove up to the hospital, where I walked into the emergency room without an apparent medical problem. I registered at the window and was asked to wait until my name was called, which I did for two hours. I was considered a non-emergency because I wasn't bleeding, clutching my heart, or disoriented. Those who were real emergencies were positioned in front of me in the waiting line.

"What were you drinking?" the nurse asked me with apparent disgust.

"Tomato juice," I responded.

"What was in the tomato juice?" she continued.

"I don't know. That's why I'm here," I said sternly.

"What is it you're wanting, Ms. Thompson?" asked the confused nurse,

"Ma'am, I lost two days. I have no idea what I did or what happened to me. I did not drink any alcohol, and I did not knowingly take any drugs, but I still lost two days. I need to find out why I lost those two days. Perhaps a quick check-up here and a blood test could help me figure out why I lost two days," I said, as honestly as I could manage without raising my voice or losing my temper.

"All right, come this way and Dr. Newsome will check you out. You will probably have to explain all of this to him when you talk with him, Ms. Thompson," she said. She seemed to accept what I had been saying.

The nurse was correct. I did have to repeat everything to Dr. Newsome, who accepted it without a problem.

The doctor checked everything that was necessary and drew several tubes of blood to be tested.

"I will get an answer today on most of the tests, but the toxicology tests will take a few days," Dr. Newsome told me.

"Dr. Newsome, do you have any idea of why I blacked out completely for two days?" I asked hoping he could give me a guess.

"Sounds like the date rape drug, but you were out much longer than normal. You may have been given a second dose, or something else in addition; perhaps a sedative of some kind. Were the people you were with friends?" he asked.

"I thought so," I answered softly, thinking about whom I was talking with when I lost track of the world and everyone in it.

"I guess I am lucky. I wasn't raped or robbed, or even killed. Someone thought enough about me to get me into a room in a motel so I could safely sleep this whole ordeal through to the end," I said to Dr. Newsome.

"Whether you know it or not, you did have a friend. Most of the people I see going through the ER are in pretty serious condition," said Dr. Newsome.

"How long will it take to get the results from the blood tests?" I asked.

"A week to ten days; I'm sending them to a lab in North Carolina. They'll do the best job of tracing the toxin," he explained.

"Will you call me when you get the results?" I asked.

"Yes ma'am, I sure will," answered Dr. Newsome.

I thought the best way for me to figure out what happened to me on Friday night was to return to the scene of the crime

Donnie's Place was a restaurant and bar combination, frequented mostly by the upper-crust and well-moneyed of this small town. Neighborhood bars were not known to exist in our small town, because the town was located in the Bible Belt. You could find a church on each street corner, but the establishments that served liquor were few and far between. It was my thinking that the Bible Belters preferred that you imbibe behind your own closed doors, away from public scrutiny.

I was starved. I had no idea when I had last eaten, and it was lunch time.

Donnie's Place was a family-owned endeavor. The entire staff, from cooks to servers to bartenders, were born or married into the family. It was a close knit bunch, so I didn't know if I was going to get very far with the questions I had to ask in my search for answers.

Donnie was the father for whom the place was named, but was no longer among the living.

Harold, his eldest son, took over the reins of control and led the business from a family-style restaurant that was drowning in debt, to a thriving dinner club, with alcoholic beverages being served to those who ordered.

Harold changed the menu because he wanted to attract the moneyed populace, and he did so with the addition of a chef who was paid big money to prepare fancy dishes that didn't appear on the menu for Hardee's or McDonald's.

Of course, the overhead for running the establishment increased tenfold, so he raised the menu prices to match and exceed the bills.

The high prices brought in the people with the big bucks, and all of the trouble that came along with them.

Harold wanted to make a profit, but he was also a peace keeper. He wanted no trouble, but he wouldn't back away if it came his way.

I entered Donnie's Place alone, which was usually the case. I was seated at a table in the corner, where I could see the entire dining room and its occupants. I ordered the high-priced, high-class hamburger platter, and dug in with glee when they set it before me. Like I said, I was starved.

When the bill was served on the fancy little tray, I asked to speak to Harold.

"Is there a problem?" asked the concerned server.

"No, nothing, everything was just fine. I need to ask Harold a question, that's all," I said, trying to calm her concern.

The server smiled and said, "I'll go find him and send him to speak with you."

A few minutes passed, and Harold presented himself to me with my change from paying the bill.

"What can I do for you, Molly?" he asked with a big, broad smile.

"You were here Friday evening," I said as a statement, not a question.

"Yes, so were you," he replied.

"I know this is going to sound strange, but can you tell me who I left with? Or did I leave alone?" I whispered so no other set of ears could hear what I had to say.

"You left alone, like you always do," he answered softly.

"Was I walking okay?" I probed.

"What do you mean?" he asked.

"I ended up in a motel in Claypool Hill and I don't know how I got there," I said with a sigh.

"You were showing signs of being tired, definitely not drunk. You didn't drink any alcoholic beverages that I'm aware of at any time," said Harold.

"I looked tired, that's what you said," I repeated his statement back to him and paused to think.

"Yes, but I didn't think anything of it. Someone else left just after you did. You were moving under your own power, so I knew you wouldn't allow anyone to bother you. At least, you never have since I've known you. You are fierce when you're attacked by anyone. I've seen you in action with a couple of bothersome drunks," said Harold.

"What did the person who followed me look like?" I continued.

"Actually, it was a lady," Harold said.

"Really? A lady? Who?" was all I could sputter. It never occurred to me that it could have been a woman.

"She's only been here a couple of times, but she seemed to know you. She talked to you for quite a while. When you left she was only a couple of seconds behind you," he explained.

"Do you remember what she looked like?" I probed.

"Yeah, I think so," he said as he closed his eyes for a moment. "She had brown hair going to gray, bright blue, sparkling eyes, and she was of average build. She was about five-five and left a good tip for the server. I guess that's why she was so well-remembered," he added.

"Thanks, Harold," I said.

Bright, blue, sparkling eyes was a good description that ought to tell me who it was I talked with. Why couldn't I remember her?

I left for home, a shower, and some fresh clothes. I was going to return to Donnie's Place to do some more investigating, but I needed to wait until dark, when the right people came out of their homes to greet their cohorts for play time.

My little house, as lonely as it could be at times, summoned me to its cozy warmth and protection. All thoughts of my night visitor had escaped my mind. It didn't seem like my problem had been the motorcycle gang member, because I was still among the living.

Living alone was a blessing most of the time, with all of the freedom to do what I wanted to do when I wanted to do it. The drawback was the loneliness that snatched all of the good reasons for solitude away from me, and I was left wanting to hear another voice not my own or escaping from the television.

Most of the time the loneliness made an appearance in the evening. That was when I went in search of real people, with whom I could exchange a few words.

I was amazed at how tired I had become. With all of the sleeping I had done for two days, I found it hard to believe I needed another nap.

I sat on the edge of my bed, telling myself I was just going to rest for a moment. Before long, I was stretched out and sound asleep.

When I awoke, the night had settled in. I could feel the pull of the night people at Donnie's Place and the need to find some answers.

I pulled into the parking lot and checked out the vehicles already parked. It looked like the same vehicles that were present on Friday when I entered the place, and no sign of any motorcycle. Of course, as with all bars, there were regulars, those who could call Donnie's Place their home away from home.

I plastered a smile to my lips and walked through the door without a care in the world. At least, that's what I wanted the patrons to see.

Because I didn't want to return to the world of the drinker, which I had visited a lot in my twenties and thirties, I ordered a Virgin Mary and proceeded to mingle with the night people.

I spoke with the barflies, the ones who called the place home, and moved on to some of the casual customers. They were more my style. I didn't want to call Donnie's Place home.

Again, I was trying to establish the whereabouts of Tim Walker, but nobody wanted to part with that information. It was either because they didn't know, or because they knew and they didn't want me to know. Whatever the reason, I was still going to continue to ask.

I was about to give up and go home when I saw her.

She was busy talking to one of the local judges. Their conversation looked intense, but friendly.

I sat at the bar and surveyed the establishment after most of the patrons had departed, including the judge.

Blue Eyes rose from her seat at the empty table and strolled up to the bar next to me.

"Molly, how are you?" she asked me.

"Fine, and I think I have you to thank," I replied with a smile.

"You needed help, and I was more than willing to take the time," said Blue Eyes.

"Could you tell me why I needed the help?" I asked as I searched her sparking, blue eyes.

"You were drugged." She answered calmly, as if it was a common, everyday occurrence.

The straightforward, blunt answer caught me off guard.

"By whom?" I demanded, when my ability to speak returned.

"Actually, it was an accident. The drug was meant for someone else," she explained.

"Why?" I snapped.

"It's a game between a man and a woman, both of whom are friends of mine. Friday night, when it became apparent that their little game had gone awry, they asked me to help you get yourself to safety. I put you in your car and I drove you to the nearest motel, where I knew you would be safe. My friends followed me, so I would have a ride back to my car. They helped me get you inside the motel room, where you were slapped around a bit. Then we all went on our separate paths," she said as if she were relating a simple rumor.

"Who did that to me? Why did they beat me?" I demanded.

"I'm not going to tell you. Just know it wasn't intentional. They panicked when they found out you were not part of the game. They wanted you to think you had been mugged," she said.

"I will eventually figure it out," I said defiantly.

"I'm sure you will, but by that time, you will have cooled off enough so there won't be a reason to carry this further, to retaliation," Blue Eyes said, in a calming voice.

"Okay, okay, but the reason I came here Friday night was to find out what has happened to my friend, Tim Walker. Since you seem to know so much, maybe you could tell me. I thought the drugging and beating was a result of my questions. Was it?" I probed.

"Not because of the questions, as far as I know. Your friend, Tim Walker, is in a rehabilitation program for a prescription drug problem. That's what no one wanted to tell you," Blue Eyes answered.

"I didn't know he had a drug problem," I sputtered.

"Most people didn't know, and it is hoped that it remains that way. Do you understand what I'm saying?" Blue Eyes asked.

I looked into those sparkling, blue eyes and said, "No one will hear it from me."

"Good," Blue Eyes as she turned to leave.

"One more question," I said as I reached to her arm to stop her walking progress.

"What's that?" she said with a smile.

"What's your name?" I asked.

"Everyone just calls me Blue Eyes. It's easier that way," she said softly.

"What's easier?" I asked.

"It's easier than trying to explain to people about someone you will never be able to find. I only show up when I'm needed. Goodbye, Molly," Blue Eyes said. Then she was gone.

"Harold," I said loudly, to attract his attention. "Did you see the lady with the sparkling blue eyes?"

"Yes," he answered.

"What is her name?" I asked.

"Don't know. We call her Blue Eyes," he said.

"How often does she come in here?" I asked.

"Not very. She told me she stops in only when she's needed," Harold answered.

I sat there staring at my drink, wondering if everyone and everything was real, or if I was gone off into a dream state.

"Molly?" shouted Harold.

"Yeah," I answered.

"I'm getting ready to close up. Do you need anything else?" he asked.

"No thanks, Harold, I'm going home to think about what Blue Eyes told me, so I can try to understand it. See you soon," I said. I grabbed my handbag and raced to the door.

When I repeated her words over and over again, I realized I had been talking to an angel called Blue Eyes, who was more than willing to lead me onward and upward to safety.

CHAPTER 22
JUST PLAIN PARANOID

Blue Eyes was the first real angel I had ever met. It seemed to me that the angels I encountered in my life were not discouraging me from running headlong into temptation, but they were helping me out of my dilemmas.

Believe me, I was grateful for the help. But it would be so much better if I didn't get into trouble in the first place.

I'd actually thought my being drugged was the result of being attacked by the motorcycle gang member. I think I was disappointed that he wasn't the one who had brought on my current round of troubles.

I was still feeling some residual affects of whatever drug I had been given. Dizziness was lingering, but the bouts would pass quickly.

I was in my house, alone again, wondering what was going to happen next.

No one had seen any sign of a motorcycle around my house.

Was it just my vivid imagination creating this melodrama? How in the world was I going to prove that I was not going crazy?

I was so sorry I didn't get a good look at him, when that guy was beating on my door. I was too afraid to peek out the window, for fear that he would see me. Then again, maybe the man beating on my door wasn't the same one who had visited my house during the night.

God help me, but I had no answers. I didn't think I was making this whole thing up. Was I?

I started to cry. My thoughts were the culprits for the sudden onslaught of tears.

I had to get out of the house. I had to get my thoughts away from my imagination and onto real things. I needed to talk to someone, but I had no idea who that would be.

It was too late to bother Patty. She probably thought I was losing it, too.

I left all of my lights burning bright inside my house, as well as all of the lights I had on the outside. If there was anyone out there waiting to do me harm, I wanted to be able to see him clearly.

I opened my front door and paused before stepping out, so I could check out the expanse of landscape in front of me.

When I stepped onto my front porch before closing my door, I scanned all of the areas that were illuminated by the outside lights. I squinted at the darkened areas, watching for any kind of movement.

"Paranoid. Molly, you're just plain paranoid," I said. I ran to my car.

No matter how much I scolded myself for being so paranoid, I couldn't chase away the cold chills of icy fear that were running down my spine.

I couldn't get into the car fast enough. I fumbled with my key as I struggled to get it inside the tiny hole. Now was the time I wished I had an electronic key.

I jumped onto the seat, jerked the door closed, and snapped the lock so I would be the only occupant of the tan Chevy Cavalier.

I started the engine and just sat there, behind the wheel, sobbing.

"Nerves, that is all it is," I mumbled. I finally put the car into gear. I glanced in my rearview mirror, where I saw a reflection of something shiny directly behind me. I blinked my eyes and it was gone.

Had I imagined that? I must have, because it was gone. I shook my head in denial as I tried to make myself believe it was my imagination.

That's when I heard it. The sounds of a motorcycle as it raced down my street caught up with me. It was like a delayed reaction. This time, I did hear it. It was real.

Then it was gone.

I backed out of my driveway and headed for a place where I would be among people. I didn't even have to know those people. I just wanted to hear voices and see smiling faces, if I was lucky, that weren't a threat to me.

I drove to the mall and found that the Piccadilly, a cafeteria-style restaurant, was still serving. I knew they had great food, and people tended to linger and talk after finishing their meals.

I filled my tray with food I didn't really want, but I needed a reason to be there and eating dinner was an excellent reason.

Of course, I didn't know any of the people who were sitting at half of the tables in the place. I was surprised to see how busy the place was, at eight o'clock in the evening. In my small town, eight o'clock for dinner was late. We all seemed to be early risers, so dinner rolled around after five, but before seven o'clock each evening.

Most of the people were professionally dressed, meaning they had probably worked late and decided to stop in for a bite before going to bed.

I ate my food slowly as I watched the other customers who were spread out before me.

I could hear bits and pieces of conversation.

The two people closest to me were males. One of those men stayed in a conversation on his cellphone the entire time he was eating.

"She's bipolar, and she is having a bad day," the man said into the phone as he chewed his piece of meat.

I didn't hear any more of his conversation because the background music, for some reason, had gotten louder. Maybe his cellphone conversation was what prompted the louder music.

Then I realized that I was focusing on the background tunes. The songs were from my era, about thirty to forty years ago, but I hadn't noticed until I paid attention to the tunes.

Each song that played reminded me of sad times when I was drinking, and searching for love everywhere that was totally wrong.

I'd had enough sad, so I tried to refocus my mind to those around me.

I noticed that the second man who had been sitting at the same table with cellphone man ate his food and left, without any further conversation with his tablemate. Of course, cellphone man did not end his conversation to talk with his tablemate.

The waitresses were running around clearing tables as quickly as possible. One of the young ladies grabbed a broom and dustpan to start the cleanup under the empty tables. I took the broom and dustpan as a sign for me to wrap up my eating and hit the road.

I started for the door, but stopped in my tracks when I heard the motorcycle revving in the parking lot.

"Are there that many motorcycles in Maxwell? If so, why are the riders going everywhere I go?" I mumbled. I stood inside the restaurant next to the door, searching for the location of the revving.

Silence...The revving had stopped and I couldn't find a motorcycle.

"Am I going crazy?" I screamed when I climbed into my car.

Again, I wanted to cry, but I wouldn't let myself do it. I had enough of crying over something I had no control over. I needed to move on, and see my life go onward and upward to better days.

CHAPTER 23
NOBODY BELIEVES ME

When I reached home, all of the lights were still shining brightly. It appeared from the outside to be just as I had left it. There was no doubt in my mind that the same would follow suit for the inside of the house.

I closed my car door quickly, ran to my front porch, inserted the key, and discovered that the door was not locked.

I froze.

I knew I had locked that door.

I turned to run.

"Molly, it's me. Don't scream or run. Please, Molly, it's me, Patty," said a soothing voice from behind the wide open front door.

The adrenaline rush overpowered me and I screamed. I couldn't help it. It was either scream or bust.

"Stop it, Molly. It's Patty. Look at me, please. I'm sorry I scared you. I only meant to help you," Patty sputtered.

I looked at her, finally seeing her, and I reached out to hug her close.

"How did you get in?" I asked when I regained my voice.

"You told me where you hid your spare key. Remember?" Patty answered.

"Oh, yeah, I forgot," I said. I searched my mind for the recollection, but I couldn't find it.

"Let's get into the house, Molly," said Patty. She ushered me through the door.

When I walked over the threshold, my jaw dropped as I moaned in disbelief.

My house was a wreck. The sofa was overturned, drawers were emptied, and papers were scattered everywhere.

"My God," I whispered, "Did you do this, Patty?"

"No! No, I didn't. It looked like this when I got here. You didn't do this, did you, Molly?"

"No," I hissed.

"Who would do this? Is anything missing?" asked Patty.

"I guess it's the same person who has been following me. He broke into my house and nearly scared me to death. Nobody believes me, Patty. They think it's my imagination. I'm not crazy, and this guy is real. I didn't do any of this, Patty. Why would I? I didn't know you would be coming by my place, did I?" I asked in a fading voice.

"Call the police, Molly. Report this. You need to have this on record somewhere," urged Patty.

"The chief of police already thinks I'm senile," I said with a smile. "You asked me if I did this. I'm sure he would ask me the same question. I'm afraid I would not be able to answer that question again in a civil tone."

"Call him, Molly. You really need help. I'll stay here with you, until he comes and goes," said Patty.

I called the police, for whatever good that did.

When the patrol car pulled into the driveway, I met him outside and told him as much as I could: I arrived home, Patty was waiting for me, and my house had been ransacked. I didn't see anything missing, but that could change when I had a chance to put everything back where it belonged.

The officer took some photographs of the disarray and left to file a report. I knew nothing more would be done, because no one saw anything.

As the police car left my driveway I turned to Patty, who was standing next to me, and said, "That was a waste of time."

"I see what you mean," said Patty.

"If this nut wants to kill me, why doesn't he just do it?" I said loudly, to Patty's amazement.

"You don't mean that, Molly," said Patty.

"I certainly do. I'm tired of living in fear," I explained. "He needs to show his face, so I can know who is doing this to me. If this goes back five years, why did he wait so long?"

"What happened five years ago?" asked Patty.

"Before my husband died, we were involved in an incident with a motorcycle gang member who was trying to make his bones as an initiation into the gang, by killing us for flashing our headlights at him. It was getting dark, and Tommy was trying to warn an oncoming car to turn on his headlights. It was on, after that. There was a car chase, and a cop was killed in a shootout at my house. The guy who had been chasing us got away from the area, and I don't think he was ever caught for killing the police officer."

"All this happened five years ago?" Patty asked in astonishment.

"Yes, and I think it is continuing now," I said breathlessly.

"What are you going to do?" asked Patty. She looked around to see if we were alone.

"I'm going to catch this guy. I'm tired of being afraid." I said it firmly, with an upward glance pleading for help to move onward with my life.

CHAPTER 24
LET THE BATTLE BEGIN

Patty helped me set the sofa upright, and I shooed her home to get some sleep.

My mind was not going to let me sleep. It was working feverishly to devise a plan. Finally, exhaustion won the battle and I stretched out on my disheveled bed, where I went to sleep in no time.

When I awoke it was after ten AM. I couldn't remember the last time I had slept that late in the morning. My only thought was that I really must have needed that sleep.

I jumped into the shower, and exited the wet warmth with a smile on my face.

"Let the battle begin," I said loudly. I started returning all of my upturned house back into its original form.

As I straightened and put things in place, my mind whirled and turned, telling me what I needed to do.

A gun was in the forefront of my mental list of necessities.

I had never felt the need to have a gun in my permanent possession until this harassment began.

I called someone I knew from my drinking days who was in that type of business, and put in an order.

"You don't need a gun, Molly," he said in a disbelieving tome.

"I have to have a gun, and if I can't get it from you, I will get it from someone else. You need to give me the name of someone who will sell me a gun," I said sternly.

Well, that remark made him understand that I really wanted and needed that gun. Eric agreed to find me a gun and sell it to me, no questions asked.

"How long will it take?" I asked in a whisper.

"A couple of days," Eric answered.

"I'll call you day after tomorrow," I said firmly.

"You're sure about this, Molly?" Eric asked.

"I've never been more sure about anything in my life," I responded with conviction.

"Okay," said Eric.

"One step closer to an answer," I mumbled, as I disconnected the telephone.

I was going to have to avoid confrontation for a couple more days, at least until I had my gun in my hands.

I decided staying in the house was the best way for me to do that.

I scooted the back of a wooden chair up under the doorknob of each of my doors to the outside as an added precaution.

In front of each of my windows I placed something that would have to be overturned with a crash if anyone tried to crawl in through a booby-trapped window.

I retrieved a pillow and blanket from my bedroom closet and settled myself in the living room on the sofa, where I would watch television for two days.

The hours of watching television were long and didn't seem to want to end. The monotony was broken up by a couple of phone calls from Patty.

"What are you doing, Molly?" asked Patty with a worried tone.

"Waiting," I answered.

"Waiting for what?" continued Patty.

"The time to pass until I get my gun," I said in a whisper.

"A gun? Where are you getting a gun? From whom?" She questioned me in a flurry of words.

"I can't tell you that, but I am getting one for protection. That's all you need to know," I explained.

"Then what will you do?" Patty asked.

"Take care of business," I answered, in a smart-alecky tone.

"Do you want any company?" Patty asked.

"No, I don't think so. I'm not doing anything except watch television and wait. You would get really bored. I know I am," I said, with all of the sincerity I could muster.

No one else called and no one knocked on my door, for which I was grateful. I didn't want to have to explain to anyone else about what I was doing. I didn't want anyone to prevent my performing my onward and upward movement to ending this problem.

Chapter 25
THE HAPPENING

The phone call came a little earlier than I expected. I was almost afraid to answer the phone when it rang. Even though I was expecting Eric's call, I was afraid it might be my nemesis, my night visitor, my motorcycle gang member.

I didn't recognize the number that flashed on my caller ID. It could have been anyone.

"Hello?" I whispered.

"Molly, this is Eric. I got what you ordered," he said, in a rush of words.

"Good, where can I meet you?" I asked.

"This evening about seven, meet me at the convenience store on Main Street. You know which one I'm talking about, don't you?" Eric asked.

"Yes, but does it have to be that late?" I asked.

"Yeah, I got things to do. Sorry, Molly," he said apologetically.

"How much?" I asked.

"A hundred. See you at seven," he said.

I ran to the box where I kept hidden cash, pulled out a hundred dollars in twenties, and stuffed them into my jeans pocket.

"I forgot to ask about bullets. Hopefully, he'll have some with him," I mumbled. I walked back into the living room to watch television and wait.

It was only nine o'clock in the morning so I still had a few hours before I could get my hands on that gun.

The television reruns were getting on my nerves. I had seen the episodes so many times previously that I had each scene memorized.

I started dozing off, fighting to keep myself awake and alert.

Something was going to happen today. I could feel it in my bones. I didn't know if I was going to be the one to make it happen, or if I would be on the receiving end of the happening. Whatever, I wanted to be ready and I needed that gun.

My eyes closed again and I was off on a hazy trip to dreamland.

***

I was running. *Of course I was running. I was always running in my dreams.*

He was coming after me. The giant specter of a motorcycle was right on my heels, and growing in size each time I glanced backwards.

I wanted to be able to get a good look at the rider, but that wasn't going to happen. In order to continue running safely, I had to watch my steps among the pieces of debris that were spread out before me.

The debris consisted of pieces of glass, thin metal, and splintered wood. Sharp points from all of the pieces were extending into the air. I was miraculously running through the maze. I was sure that any pause in my forward movement, any hesitation at all, would cause me to step on a shiny piece of pain.

All I wanted to do was stop, turn around, and look directly at the rider of the motorcycle. All I was permitted to do was run at a constant, steady pace.

My running gait slowed a bit, and the motorcycle specter moved closer. I ducked my head and tried to run faster, but actually I slowed down a bit. I slowed enough to cause my running feet to falter, and I stepped directly onto a piece of glass that pierced my sneaker, but did not cut my foot.

I tried not to think about my running. If I did, my speed would change and a piercing would occur.

The motorcycle was looming closer, growing larger and larger.

The rider's face was becoming much clearer.

Finally, I could see him. Well, almost, because he had a full beard and a fierce looking helmet that covered his features. The only thing I was sure of about his appearance was his beard.

The long, flowing beard looked out of place. Actually, the hair from the beard looked more like head hair. It made the scene surreal.

128

The specter was moving closer, but for some unknown reason it was not catching up with me.

I wanted the rider to remove his helmet. I wanted to see his face. I wanted to find out why he was chasing me. Did he think I could testify against him in court?

All I could say was that a motorcycle rider, presumably a gang member who was going through an initiation, was chasing Tommy and me. I could only guess that he was present at the shootout at my house, because I wasn't there. The chief of police had stashed me away in the supermarket to keep me from the action.

I never did clearly see the man chasing me then, and I couldn't see him this time. So again, all I could say was, "Why?"

I was becoming breathless from all of the running. Then something truly strange happened.

The specter came close enough to me that I could almost touch him, even though I was running as fast as I could through the debris field.

I turned my head to reach for him, but he was gone. I was left staring into the darkness of the night.

***

I was startled awake and covered with sweat from running. My coverlet had been shoved to the floor, and I was positioned with my head hanging over the arm of the sofa.

I needed to write down the details of my dream in my journal. No, it was a nightmare.

"What good would that do," I mumbled. I threw the pen and paper across the room. "Molly, it was only a dream," I told myself angrily. "You've got to move onward and upward, and writing the events of a dream isn't helping you do that."

129

CHAPTER 26
UNFINISHED BUSINESS

I had made it to three in the afternoon. I still had four more hours to while away, before I would meet Eric.

In my minds eye, the specter from my nightmare planted itself firmly in my thoughts.

Other than the fact that there was a helmeted motorcycle rider in both scenarios, (the first one chasing Tommy and me, and the second chasing only me) I could identify nothing or no one else.

Why did this guy feel the need to end my last days on this earth?

In my mind, I finally found the answer to that question.

I was unfinished business.

I should have died five years earlier, when it was his assignment to kill the good Samaritan of the highway. In my case, the good Samaritan was Tommy. I imagine he earned his way into the gang with the death of the law officer, even though that was not his original goal.

It would become my goal, if I wanted to enjoy my waning years, to prevent him from attaining his goal, which was my death.

My phone rang and jolted me out of my thoughts.

"Hello?" I said as I read blocked on the caller ID.

"Molly Thompson, you are going to die," whispered an ugly voice.

"Yes, someday but not today," I answered angrily. I slammed down the phone. I picked it up again to check to see if I had broken the instrument.

I put the receiver up to my ear to listen for the dial tone, but it was silent. No irritating buzz could be heard. Instead, I heard crackling noises as if the phone was off the hook in another room. Then total silence.

I knew it couldn't be off the hook anywhere else, because I only had one extension.

Then I realized that someone could be messing with the outside junction box. That meant the house phone was disabled, so I searched for my cellphone in my handbag. I had forgotten to charge that piece of equipment, and it was totally out of juice. I hooked it up to the charger and dialed Patty's number.

It rang and rang, but there was no answer. My first thought was that she was running an errand or two. I dialed her cellphone number. I needed to talk with someone, and Patty was my best someone, my best friend. Again, there were several rings before I was routed to voice mail.

"Patty, I need to talk with you. Call me as soon as you get this. I have a problem," I said. I disconnected my line.

"Now what?" I wondered out loud.

I turned off my television and listened for strange noises. I had every entry, door or window, into my house booby trapped. No one would be able to get in without my hearing the racket he would make.

I knew he was near. I could feel him, but he hadn't made it into my house yet.

He was able to prevent me from using my land line, but he didn't have the jamming mechanism required for my cellphone.

I was straining with every ounce of energy within me to listen for strange sounds. I was so focused on listening that the sudden burst of sound from my cellphone startled me.

"Hello," I whispered into my cell, after checking to see what number the call was made from.

"Molly? Are you okay?" asked Patty.

"No, he's right outside my house. He's already cut the wire for my house phone. I'm expecting him to break in at any moment," I said, with fear etched in my voice.

"Have you called the police?" Patty asked.

"No, no, I wanted to talk with you first. I think I know why this is happening. If anything happens to me, please tell the police chief for me," I explained.

"Stop it, Molly. I'm going to hang up and call the police now," she said worriedly.

"No! Listen, Patty, this man trying to kill me is doing it because I'm unfinished business from five years ago. Just remember that for me, okay?" I whispered harshly.

There was as crash of broken glass and a rumble of overturned furniture.

"He's in the house now! Call the police!" I screamed to Patty. I hung up and cursed the fact that I didn't have a gun.

I could hear him crashing around, trying to rid himself of the tangle of furniture he had climbed into.

I always kept a baseball bat behind the sofa next to the front door, so I headed for the door.

Then, the thought that I might try to throw open the lock and run for my life occurred to me.

I grabbed the bat, positioned it between my legs, and busied my hands with unlocking the door.

"Molly. You can't leave. Not now, I just found you!" screamed an ugly male voice.

I jumped when he spoke, but the bat did not fall. I had not finished with the locks. I still had to turn the deadbolt before I could leave.

"Why are you trying to kill me? What did I ever do to you?" I asked. I tried to choke back the tears of fear that were building up inside of me.

"For me to move ahead in the gang I'm in, you must die!" he screamed at me.

"Why?" I asked choking on my words. "You killed a cop. Isn't that enough?"

"No, I was supposed to kill you and your old man. He's already dead, so I can't do anything about that now. I can kill you and wipe my slate clean," he said, waving a gun around in front of me.

"You don't have to kill me. What's your name, by the way?" I asked, hoping for more time.

"My name is Victor, and I have to kill you, Molly," he said with a snarl.

I heard another sound. I turned my head and stepped towards the window.

A bullet whizzed past my head and hit the door facing, causing it to splinter.

I grabbed my baseball bat and started swinging it as hard and as fast as I could. I felt the bat connect with something, and I heard a sickening crack.

My front door burst open, and a group of policemen entered my house with guns drawn.

Someone grabbed me. I thought it was a policeman.

I was so wrong.

I was standing in the middle of the room, with Victor holding a gun to my head. He had corralled me with his left arm, and was holding the gun in the other hand.

I moved a little and bumped his left arm, which caused him to growl with pain. I must have connected with it when I was swinging the bat. I must have broken his left arm up near the shoulder area. That bit of information was good to know.

He seemed to hook his body around me as he forced me into the space where he needed me to stand, so the cops could see the gun pointed at my temple.

I could feel him cringe with the pain of holding my body against his. He was hurting bad, but it wasn't enough to stop him from shooting me in the head.

"Put the gun down," shouted the police officer nearest to me.

Victor growled, "Back off, or she's dead."

"Put the gun down now," shouted the police officer again, with much more force.

"She'll die if you don't get out of my way," Victor snarled.

I was not the bravest person in the world, but I knew I was going to be dead no matter which way he chose to go.

If they let us walk out, Victor was going to kill me regardless. If it became a standoff to the end, he would put a bullet in my brain before they killed him. This was a lose-lose situation, no matter how I looked at it.

I hoped Patty would remember what I told her, so she could tell the police chief what had actually happened.

I felt Victor tense up again. The pain was probably doing that to him. I decided when I felt him clench the next time from a surge of pain, I would make my move. Exactly what that would be, I didn't have a clue.

The police officers were getting impatient, and I was getting more and more scared. I had very little time left. Victor was getting impatient, too.

I could feel him finger the trigger, and I thought I was a goner.

"Victor," I said. "You don't want to die, do you?"

"They're not going to let me live," he whispered to me harshly.

"Yes, they will, as long as you don't give them a reason to shoot you," I said in a whisper.

"Lady, I killed a cop. I won't live long enough to go to jail," he snarled.

"Yes you will. I know most of these cops, and I know they will do the right thing," I continued.

"Shut up, Molly. You don't know what you're talking about," he growled, flinching from pain.

"Yes, I do," I said. I bent over quickly, while pushing against his injured arm. I fell to the floor, holding my eyes tightly closed.

A shot rang out, and I wasn't sure if I was hit or not. I lay there on the floor, too afraid to move a muscle.

Maybe it was a stupid thing to do. All I knew for sure was that if I didn't do something, anything, I was a dead woman.

The police chief came running at me and swept me up off of the floor like I was a rag doll.

"Brian, I'm okay. At least, I think I'm okay. Nothing is hurting me except my pride," I said, as I tried to steady myself on my feet.

"Why should your pride be hurting? You're the one who actually caught this guy," said Brian. He looked at me to determine if all of my parts were where they were supposed to be. "How could you have known that this went all the way back to five years ago?"

"Just a hunch, an intuition, and the motorcycle," I said calmly.

"You had to have seen a lot of motorcycles since that day. Why now?" asked Brian.

"The motorcycle was parked behind my house. I know of no one who would have the right to park their bike behind my house," I said sternly.

"We didn't find anything when we checked out your house, the day you said you saw the bike," said Brian.

"I know, but that didn't mean that it wasn't there earlier. You just didn't find it, that's all," I said, almost apologetically. I didn't want him to think he had done anything wrong. The motorcycle simply wasn't there, so they dropped the search for any signs of a trespasser.

"Molly, I need you to go to the police station to make a statement about what has happened over the past few days. Are you up to that?" asked the police chief.

"Can I do it tomorrow?" I asked, looking directly at him.

"Sure, no problem, but you can't stay here tonight. Have you got someone you can stay with?" asked Brian.

"My best friend, Patty, if she will have me," I said, as I looked at her. She had appeared by my side during the aftermath. I had no idea when she arrived, but I sure was glad to see her because I knew she would help me move onward and upward to returning to a normal life.

CHAPTER 27
IT'S FINALLY OVER

I sat in Patty's living room, drinking a cup of hot tea, munching on a cookie, and watching my best friend take care of me.

We talked about the events of this story that had to be filled in by others. The chief of police let me know about other events, a lot of which I had not been a direct part. Of course Patty told me everything she'd discovered or knew. Most of it, however, came from me and how I managed to interpret the clues to the puzzle of life.

I always knew the motorcycle gang member would reappear somewhere in my life. Again, it was a gut feeling, an intuition, and I guess I was right. Maybe all of that déjà vu mumbo jumbo hadn't left me completely.

Patty and I had become close, best buddies really, after my husband died. I was alone and getting through the long, long evenings were very difficult for me.

I tried all of the usual pastimes, such as; stopping at the malls, which cost too much money because I always felt the need to buy something if I spent much time in a specific store; volunteering for organizations that I thought would help me accumulate friends; and church functions that occurred only two days a week. Even though each of those functions helped in its own way, I was still so alone every evening.

I would go to work and I was so very grateful for having a job, but come workday end I would go home to the lonely, empty house.

At Tommy's funeral, Patty told me she would call me that evening. She did call me, and I was so surprised that she took the time or even remembered to give me a call. When we ended our first conversation, she told me she would call me the next evening, if I didn't mind.

Did I think that would happen? No way.

I was so surprised when that second phone call came, and each phone call for each evening thereafter.

I was so moved by her phone calls that I wrote an article, a public thank you note, to be submitted to a national publication in the hopes that it would be printed to let others know how important a simple phone call can be to a person who is hurting and alone.

PATTY–MY EVERYDAY HERO

"I'll call you later," said Patty, as she squeezed my hand to comfort me.

I looked into her eyes and thanked her for her kindness, but I really didn't expect her to spend her time giving me a call.

I remember yearning for time to be alone without distractions. My house had been filled with as many as six people living under my roof, but with the recent death of my husband of twenty-five years, I became the sole occupant of my household.

Now, the idea of being alone all the time led me to tears most every night. Then it was off to bed, to sleep through the loneliness.

I would gladly get out of bed each morning to go to work, where I would at least be near people. I didn't have to be in constant contact with anyone in particular, I just needed to know someone was within shouting distance. I needed to know there was a presence of someone.

I would stop at the grocery store or dollar store on my way home so I didn't have to go into my empty house, but that was getting expensive. I felt compelled to purchase something every time I passed time in the stores, and I just couldn't afford to do that anymore.

Patty called me every evening.

"Hey, Molly, how are you doing?" She asked each time I answered the welcomed ring.

"Fine," I replied automatically. "How are you?"

"I'm good," she responded. "Are you sure you're fine?"

"Yes, but I'm so glad and thankful you called, Patty," I said, in a tear-filled voice.

"You're welcome. I'll call again tomorrow, okay?" she asked, with concern etched in her voice. "If you ever need anything, please call me, Molly,"

"Sure, okay, Patty, I will. Goodbye, and thank you again for calling."

Every time she called, I always felt better; like I was no longer alone in the world.

As soon as the happy friendly feeling faded, I would get ready for bed. The noise from the television would lull me to sleep, and drown out the scary sounds of the world outside my bedroom window.

Each evening I would go home from work and wait for my phone call from Patty. I'm sure she had no idea how important those phone calls were to me.

Patty threw me a lifeline every night, and kept me from sinking to be lost forever in the depression brought on by loneliness.

More than six years have passed since that first phone call. They continue to come most every evening. A majority of the time, the only communication we share is that nightly phone call. We do not visit each other's home and seek physical comfort in the form of a big hug; instead the telephone is our hug for each other. I can feel her warm, friendly hug with each phone call.

Patty will forever be my everyday hero.

***

I don't think anyone in this world could ever convince me that Patty was not an angel. She'd been my angel, my beacon, and my friend for over six years. If you didn't happen to see her the same way that I did, then I guess you've not had the opportunity to experience a true friendship. She would do anything for me if I asked, but that was what was so special about her. I needed to ask. She would not force her kind deeds upon me.

It was odd when I thought about it, but my dad was much the same way. If I sought his help, he was more than willing to give it to me. He did not interfere in my life, nor did he try to control me after I became an adult. It was my life to live.

I guess maybe I've had two strong angels in my life, but I wasn't aware of it until now. My life continues moving onward and upward, in my quest to show all the people I can—ANGELS ARE EVERYWHERE.

ABOUT THE AUTHOR

Linda Hudson Hoagland of Tazewell, Virginia, a graduate of Southwest Virginia Community College, has won acclaim for her series of novels including *Snooping Can Be Doggone Deadly, Snooping Can be Devious, Snooping Can Be Contagious, Snooping Can Be Dangerous, The Best Darn Secret, An Awfully Lonely Place, The Backwards House, Death by Computer, Checking on the House,* and *Crooked Road Stalker.* She has also written biographies and stage plays and has had her short stories, essays, and poems published in anthologies including *Cup of Comfort* and *Christmas Blooms.* Her other books include *Watch Out for Eddy, Just a Country Boy: Don Dunford–Updated 2014, Living Life for Others, Quilted Memories, 90 Years and Still Going Strong,* a selection of short writings entitled *A Collection of Winners,* and a poetry collection *I Am...Linda Ellen.*

Linda Hudson Hoagland is the 2015 President of the Appalachian Authors Guild.

Hoagland is a retired Tazewell County School Board Purchase Order Clerk where she worked for almost 23 years.

She has two sons, Mike and Matt who are married to Sherry and Becky.

For more information, visit www.lindasbooksandangels.com or email lhhoagland@yahoo.com.

AWARDS

1st Place – Pearl S. Buck Award for Writing for Social Change
West Virginia Writers

1st Place – Sherwood Anderson Short Story Contest

1st Place – Summertime Blues Poetry Contest –
The Storyteller Magazine (Arkansas)

2nd Place – On the Same Page Literary Contest (North Carolina)

3rd Place – Alabama Writers Conclave – Creative Nonfiction

3rd Place – Green River Writers Flash-Fiction Contest – Kentucky

4th Place – Alabama Writers Conclave – Short Story

Honorable Mention – Writer's Digest Popular Fiction Awards/Crime (National)

Honorable Mention – The Writers' Workshop Hard Times Contest
(North Carolina)

Publication – Poetry Society of Tennessee Northeast Chapter's Anthology –
Fresh Breath

Honorable Mention – Tennessee Mountain Writers –
Inspirational Writing

Bluestone Review – Published a poem and short story

Kudzu – Published a short story

COMING SOON

Look for *Missing Sammy* also written by Linda Hoagland. In this fact-based fictional novel, Hoagland follows the path of Ella Hutchins as she steps onto the road of living again in a new life, without her other half.

Ella returns to being the strong Appalachian women she knew she was, when she undergoes a life-altering change.

www.ingramcontent.com/pod-product-compliance
Lightning Source LLC
Chambersburg PA
CBHW051839170626
46807CB00003B/1256